To Betty and Grail

"It's life O'Clock
and all is well!"

Thank you for
your love and
your friendship

Jay

El Seréno

*a short epic
novel*

Jay Frankston
Cover by Bettina Lewis Sluzki

By the same author available from
Whole Loaf Publications
Little River, CA 95456
wlp@mcn.org

A CHRISTMAS STORY, a true story
THE OFFERING, a series of Meditations on the Meaning of Life
SEEDS, a Collection of Sayings and Things
THE GIRL IN THE PICTURE, and other poems

Chapbooks:
YOM HASHOAH, remembering the Holocaust
CROSSING OVER, a catalyst for change in mid-life
TALES OF MENDOCINO, Mendocino Magic
POLISHING THE DIAMOND, and other musings

Copyright © 2009
By Jay Frankston
All rights reserved

Library of Congress Control Number: 2010902584
ISBN: Hardcover   978-1-4500-5072-2
                 Softcover   978-1-4500-5071-5
                 Ebook   978-1-4500-5073-9

First Edition.

This book was printed in the United States of America.

To order additional copies of this book, contact:
Xlibris Corporation
1-888-795-4274
www.Xlibris.com
Orders@Xlibris.com
56707

To my beautiful Granddaughters
Ilana and Erica
with love

EL SERÉNO

*This novel is a work of fiction. Most of the
historical background is authentic and much
that is written about the Serenos of Spain is
accurate but it remains a work of fiction.*

CHAPTER 1

THE RAIN HAD STOPPED. The night thread a black ribbon through the narrow streets of the old section of Madrid and the darkness was sliced open here and there by the yellow light from sparse lamp-posts that left many dense shadows in doorways and corners. The cobblestones glistened where the light reached and the silence lay thick all around. It was as if the rain had lulled the world to sleep and, having done so, it had lapsed into a heavy hush.

Suddenly, the silence was broken by a clap-clap somewhere in the street, somewhere in the night. The buildings tightly crouched together carried the echo of the clap around corners, in and out of doorways, and when it abated, the silence returned, heavier than before. Moments went by moments that, in that silence, were stretched like a spider's web all the way to infinity.

Then, clap-clap, it came again, louder still, almost annoyed at having to repeat itself. And the resonance vibrated from wall to wall, from street to street. Then the quiet took over again. But there was anxiety in the silence, a waiting somewhere. Then a voice boomed "SERENO" loud and sonorous, like an opera singer's, as if the word had come out of the deep cavern of an open mouth whose face belonged to no one. In the silence that followed the man stood before the portal, shuffling back and forth, impatient, annoyed, till he shouted out "SERENO" once again, this time louder still, with a slight question mark at the end, as if to ask "Where are you?". Then at a loss, unprepared for such an eventuality, the man walks out of the flickering light of the lamp-post into the darkness and toward the corner, searching, his walk heavy and undirected, almost confused.

All at once he trips and nearly falls on a large mass lying there on the wet pavement. In the dark the mass takes the form of an elongated potato sack but, as he looks closer, he sees the man, lying face down, motionless. With both hands he turns him over and the clang, clang, clanging of the keys tells him who it is. He reaches in his pocket for a match and strikes it. In the soft glow, the Sereno's face appears. It is an old weathered face with leathered skin and a remnant of hair still thick and dark in places. The lines, the thin lips, the wrinkled brow all attest to timeless age, ageless time. He strikes another match and the flicker is reflected in the open deep-sunken eyes whose light has gone out. Yet there is a sense of mystery and knowing that remains, as if the soul had not left the man yet though the life had gone out of him.

The old Sereno was dead. He died where he lived, there, in the night, in the street, in the shadow, with the keys dangling from his neck, like an actor who died on stage.

*   *   *

MADRID WAS ON FIRE. It was 1974 and the Civil War had been over for thirty-five years yet it simmered in the background and the bitterness erupted on the streets of Spain as if it had only been yesterday. Francisco Franco still held the reins of power firmly in his grip. Though old and sick now the Caudillo kept the lid on tight, supported by the small upper middle-class he had favored, by the church, and by a segment of the people who had remained blindly loyal to him over the years.

Madrid was on fire. The blaze was not above ground but it was there just the same, a violent unrest which ran through the streets and into the cafés. There the intelligentsia gathered in small groups and plotted demonstrations which would break out in front of government buildings, in factories, or at the University. Those whose lives had been sweetened by a cushiony administration job, or who had inherited power and were bent on holding on to it, were getting desperate. So the Guardia Civil, in their green uniforms and three-cornered hats, came down heavy on students and workers alike, smashing heads and arresting anyone who spoke out against the government.

Madrid was on fire. The people had simmered under the boot for too long and the Spanish temperament, wild like the wind, like the bulls whose blood runs red and passionate on Sundays in the Plaza de Toros, exploded everywhere. When a student named Hernando was shot to death during a demonstration, the walls of the city screamed in anger "Hernando, hermano, no te olvidaremos!" "Muerte al fascismo!"

Despite it all Madrid was alive. Bustling by day on the boulevards and in the shops fast-paced Madrillenos sought to quench their thirst for the good life by whatever means were available. After hours, tall modern buildings emptied their businessmen and bureaucrats and poured them into nearby cafés for some tapas and a vaso de vino before going home. It was hectic.

BUT IN THE OLD SECTION of the city, the old town, the barrio as they called it, things were quiet and hadn't changed in many a hundred years. The narrow cobble-stoned streets thread their way around blind corners, lined on both sides with huge portals ornately decorated with lions or gargoyles carved into the wood some centuries ago.

During the daytime the doors were open, occasionally revealing small well-tended courtyards with a sculpture or a water fountain in the middle, and flowers on every window sill. Rickety old staircases led up to living quarters which had been inhabited by diverse generations of Spaniards, from the very rich who owned all the buildings and had servants and caretakers, to families who shared the space as a compound which had been divided into apartments for six to eight families. The days were soft and flowing but the night cleared the streets and everything seemed hushed and rolled up until morning.

When one who lived behind one of those portals came home late at night he would be locked out. The guardera was off after 10 P.M. and the resident was always without a key. He would clap his hands twice and the clap would echo through the street and disappear into the darkness and out of that darkness would come the shadow of a man with a large metal ring around his neck and a quantity of heavy keys dangling from it. Without looking he would fumble among them and quickly come up with the right one which he would stick into the keyhole and, as if by magic, the door would open. A few pesetas in the outstretched hand, a gently whispered "Gracias Señor" and the man would disappear into the night, the softly clanging sound trailing behind him.

He was called "the Sereno" and he worked the streets from ten at night until six in the morning covering some fifteen square blocks, which was as far as the echo would carry the clap clap of the locked out house-dweller. He was one of many who walked the streets at night in all the old sections of all the old cities of Spain. They were not hired by the city or anyone else for that matter. They all came from the same small town in the north, worked for tips, and passed the keys down from generation to generation, each Sereno covering an area to which he belonged and, in a sense, which belonged to him. This was more than just a feeling from the familiarity of the sector. He knew every nook and cranny, every brass knocker on every door, every flower pot on every window sill, every lace curtain and the heavy breathing of those who slept or made love behind them. He knew the cobble stones that were broken and the ones that stuck up here and there. He could count the steps between the widely spaced lamp posts which cast a yellow gleaming light and left the in-between in semi-darkness. He knew the stray dogs that howled at night when the moon was full. It was from their howling that he knew it, for the moon could not be seen through the narrow slit that the roofs of the houses formed and only a thin strip of sky was visible. He knew the cats that slinked in the alleys and screeched and fought over scraps found in odd garbage deposits in a doorway somewhere.

Above all he knew the people, the inhabitants of the barrio, the ones who lived there and whom he served. He knew them well, almost intimately you might say. He knew their habits and their ways, their dress and their demeanor, who did what, when and with whom. He heard them yell at each other in domestic squabbles that echoed through the neighborhood. He heard them sing and make music into the night when the streets were bare and their laughter would rip through the silence. And in the often quiet night when all was still, he heard them breathe, or snore, or wake up screaming when the nightmare struck.

They never wondered why, when the double clap left their hands, it never took more than an instant for the Sereno to appear. They took it for granted that he was there somewhere in the darkness, waiting for them key in hand. They never considered that he could be fifteen narrow streets away and that it might take him some time to get to them. Because he never was and it never did. He knew them. When they left, where they went, what cantina waylaid them for how many drinks, what wall they would stop and urinate against before showing up half-cockeyed in front of their portal. And he'd be there, in the shadow, waiting for them to put those hands together and clap.

The years had made them old friends, as familiar as each cobble stone on the cobble-stoned streets. Each detail of their lives had somehow leaked into the street, into his street, into the night, into his night. And he stood there waiting in the shadow with his bastion, his chuzo, his staff or cane, at the bottom of which was a sharp metal tip which made a crisp sound as he tapped his chuzo twice upon the pavement to announce to some house-dweller that he had heard the clap and was on his way. It also served him well when, as happened on occasion, a night crawler, thief or burglar, would invade his territory to do his mischief. He would chase after him, bastion in hand, the sharp point aimed, like the charge of the cavalry, flagging his other arm and shouting loud and long. What devil would not be frightened by this little man, whose features were barely discernible in the dark, who came on like a mother bat protecting its young.

It was his barrio. His! It belonged to him and to his father before him. Yes! It had always been that way. They had all come from Asturias to be Serenos in this, his barrio. Way back, well over a hundred years ago, they had walked the night singing out hourly "It's two o'clock and all is well", "Son las dos y Sereno". That's where, in time, he got his name. The Sereno, the one who walks the night and watches and cares.

The amazing thing, by contrast, is that no one knew his name. No one ever asked. They didn't know where he came from, who he was or where he lived. No one paid much attention to him. He just lived in the night and it swallowed up his identity and left him standing in a doorway, a shadow with a ring of keys around his neck. And now the shadow had fallen and lay there on the bare pavement lifeless. The Sereno was dead.

CHAPTER 2

THE EARLY MORNING SUNSHINE came streaming through the open French windows of the Elders' conference room on the second floor of the barrio's community hall. The light splattered across the highly polished table whose legs were carved lion's paws and whose length stretched from one end of the room to the other. On both sides were tall, thin, leather-upholstered chairs. The long wall was lined with bookcases from floor to ceiling, stacked with musty old books wherein the births, communions, marriages and deaths of the barrio's residents were duly recorded in the slow and meticulous hand of Carlos, the old town recorder. And he stood there, his back against the shelves, as if he were holding them up. Two of the elders, one tall and lanky the other short and stocky, stood by the open window looking down upon the street and the street cleaner, broom in hand, methodically sweeping litter into a pan. A third man stood on the far end reading La Prensa and scratching the back of his head with one hand. Yet another sat at the table resting his head between his hands. The door opened and a well-dressed elderly gentleman came in.

"Buenos dias Señores" he sing-songed gravely. The five men almost snapped to attention in deference to the obvious command and seniority of the new arrival.

"Buenos dias Don Donato" they replied in a chorus.

"You all know why we are here this morning" he said setting down an old leather satchel and taking a seat at the center of the long wooden table. The elders nodded and quickly took seats as if they had been assigned to them. They were all men in their fifties and sixties, in suits that were either too big or too small for them and ties they were obviously not used to. But each preserved his individuality in some small way by a cap or a Basque beret or a decoration on a lapel indicating service and heroism in some long forgotten war.

Don Donato pulled out a silver case from his coat pocket and offered cigars all around. Then he bit off the end, spat it into the copper bowl at his feet, lit the cigar and took a long draw into his lungs, leaning back into his chair. "So now, let's see" he asked "what was his name?" The elders looked at each other but the question just hung there over the table. Don Donato turned to the man on his left, the one with the Basque beret tilted to one side.

"Eduardo?" he asked.

"Señor?"

"What was his name?" he repeated.

Eduardo was a small man but the question seemed to make him smaller. "I don't know" he stammered.

Don Donato looked at the others questioningly but each in turn shook his head from side to side. "Carlos, you are the recorder, you must know who he was?" The question was pointed and Carlos felt stung by it but he had no answer. Don Donato rose to his feet and walked toward the open window, staring out and blowing large puffs of smoke from his cigar into the fresh morning air. His annoyance at the missing name was tempered by the realization that he didn't know the name of his Sereno either. In any case the name of the man didn't matter. The question was what to do now.

Don Donato turned abruptly. "Didn't he have a son, or a cousin, or even a nephew who could take over for him?" The men shrugged their shoulders and remained silent. "Que lastima!" he said throwing his hands up. "We now have a problem."

Don Donato walked back to the table, hefted the satchel unto the chair and took out the large metal ring with eighty or so long keys on it, each notched differently and shaped with indents and swirls. He laid them on the table and the men gathered around and stared. They were bewildered. They had not been faced with anything like this in all their years on the elders' council. Who was going to take over for the old Sereno and how was he to figure out which key fit which door.

They were lost in thought when Don Donato called them to attention. He had a commanding personality and the elders respected his authority. "I've given it some thought. We will put an advertisement in La Prensa and find some young man to take the Sereno's place" he announced. He turned to the short one whose stomach bulged out of his pants. "Guillermo", he said, "you are the secretary. You see to it that La Prensa gets an ad for a Sereno from the Council of the Elders."

"Si Señor" Guillermo replied obediently. "I'll get to it right away."

"In the meantime, the portals of the barrio will remain open until we find a replacement". Don Donato straightened up. "Well gentlemen, that concludes our business for the day. Adios Señores", and, leaving the keys on the table, Don Donato took the satchel and walked out.

The moment he was gone the men gathered around the table and stared at the ring of keys splattered across the polished mahogany top. There was a key on that ring that opened the portal of each of the members of the Council but they had no notion which one and they tried to imagine going through the keys one at a time to find it. That fleeting though gave way to excitement and they chattered away speculating on what would happen. This was an event. This had never happened before.

*   *   *

THE AD WAS DULY PLACED in the paper as Don Donato had instructed but it produced few replies. The sector

20

that the old Sereno had worked had, over the many years, become rundown. The residents were rather poor and, since the Sereno lived on tips, there weren't many takers for so meager an income. A retired adjutant with hash marks on his sleeve offered to take on the job but he was over sixty and had arthritis and how long would he be able to be a Sereno anyway? What's more he had no children so the elders dismissed him from consideration out-of-hand. Then there was Manuel. He was a relic of a young man with fish eyes through extra-thick glasses who couldn't tell one elder from the other. How would he be able to tell one key from the other? The one with the red eyes was Roberto. He didn't know why he had answered the ad and he reeked of alcohol even though he appeared sober during the interview.

Meanwhile the portals of the barrio remained open and the residents were fretful. They double locked their doors and windows at night and pulled the blankets over their heads.

Several days later a young man presented himself to the council. His name was Ignacio. He was a young twenty-five with long curly blond hair and the intense far-away look of someone who wasn't quite there. The elders saw Ignacio's retardation and weren't put off by it. He was simple-minded they said but they didn't feel that it would hinder him as a Sereno. What's more Ignacio was anxious for the job. He really wanted it. So they gave it to him.

On a warm sunny day, some three weeks after the old Sereno had died, the elders gathered in the council chamber and, in a solemn ceremony presided over by Don

Donato, they put the ring of keys around young Ignacio's neck. Each of the elders then kissed him on both cheeks and shook his hand vigorously. Then they congratulated each other on a job well done while Ignacio, beaming from ear to ear, looked down upon the keys around his neck as if they were precious pearls, proud of the confidence these highly important men had bestowed upon him. He would honor their trust and do his job with diligence and expediency. He would be a good Sereno.

*   *   *

FOR SEVERAL MORE WEEKS the doors of the barrio remained open and the Sereno was nowhere to be seen at night. But in the daytime Ignacio wandered the streets, going from door to door, from portal to portal, trying each of the eighty some odd keys in each keyhole, finding one here and one there, jumping up and down at each find and making intricate notes on which key belonged to which gate. He did this with zest and an energy motivated by the feeling of pride and responsibility in this, his first important job. He was well acquainted with the area he was to work in. His father was an iceman and had delivered ice to the residents of the barrio. He would pull his horse and cart into the courtyard, heft a sixty pound block of ice on his shoulder and carry the huge block up the stairs to the customer. Ignacio often worked with his father so the gates and the portals were familiar to him. He had played in some of those courtyards when he was a boy. Finding the key was almost a game for him now but a game he took seriously and meant to be good at. He started every morning, going from street to street, from door to door, diligently and methodically searching to put the pieces together.

Then it was time to test his knowledge so the elders gave the word and the doors were shut and the portals were locked and Ignacio found himself walking the streets of the barrio at night waiting for the first clap-clap to call him to duty. It was a long and arduous trek. Somehow the clap-clap always seemed to come from the other end of the sector and it took him several minutes to get there. Then, in the dark, he would fumble again and again with key after key while the dweller stamped his feet impatiently till, at long last, the right key fit into the lock and the door opened to everyone's relief.

As the months went by Ignacio got better at his job. The resident's clap was answered promptly and the right key was found without hesitation. Ignacio didn't have much language skills, nor much ability to communicate but he had a good memory for names and faces and the tips improved. There was an acceptance by the people of the sector that Ignacio recognized and it gave him a sense of belonging which he had never felt.

In time each door found its key and all keys found their match. Well, almost all. That is all the keys except one. That one was different. It was longer and heavier than the others and had strange markings, jagged edges and notches all along the side. Ignacio spent many daytime hours combing through his barrio looking for a door, a portal, a gate that this last key would unlock, to no avail. Still he continued looking. It wasn't curiosity but a sense of duty to the elders who had placed their trust in him that was nagging him and egging him on. He was going to search until he found.

Little did he know that that key was the key to the old Sereno's life, the one he had succeeded and who died in total anonymity. That that key would shed a light on who he was, who he had been, and the life he had led while others slept.

CHAPTER 3

HIS NAME WAS MANÓLO GARCIA GARCIA and he was born in 1896 in Asturias on the north coast of Spain where the Cantabrian Mountains plunge down to the Bay of Biscay, a small pueblo named Cangas del Narcea, a few miles southwest of Oviedo. Manólo was the youngest of five children. Both his parents were Garcías. They were cousins. The Garcías were a large family. Manólo didn't remember his father. Pépé had left home when Manólo was only two. He had gone to Madrid to be a Sereno in one of the old barrios of the city. The rest of the family, his mother Amalia, his aunt Rosa and his sister Margo, worked the land of their few acres of corn while his three older brothers worked in the mines.

The mountainous mining region was a desolate place where the rivers run black over slate and shale. The miners were a tough hardy folk. The equipment they used was ancient and the coal they dug out was difficult to extract. But the sky over Asturias seemed higher and the sun brighter than elsewhere. The light, silver and gold threads of brilliancy, gave the town and surrounding farms a feel of vastness, of spaciousness and unending plains. There were few men in Cangas del Narcea, not in the town nor on the land. The few that were there were miners or old

JAY FRANKSTON

men who had lived their day. All the others were gone,
working in the cities as Serenos.

In the cemetery outside of town there were stray cats
who made their home in the crypts and behind broken
tomb stones. A woman they called La Vieja who lived
close by took care of them. She was in her seventies, wore
a long black coat, was heavily made up with rouge, dark
eye shadow and bright red lipstick and one could imagine
that she had been in vaudeville in her youth. Every day she
would wheel a converted baby carriage from one place to
another collecting leftovers from restaurants to feed "her"
cats. She gave them all names and came religiously every
day. She could not leave or go on vacation.

There were no vacations for Serenos either. Serenos
stayed in the city. The distance was so great and the ride so
long and expensive that most came home only once every
few years. But all sent money regularly to help the family
who was holding down the land. It was an old tradition. It
had always been that way. The young men would work on
the land or in the nearby mines, marry young, have two
or three children by the time they were twenty, and leave
the town and the family to go off to some big city like
Barcelona or Madrid to become a Sereno. All of Manólo's
brothers had left the mines and gone to be Serenos, leaving
their wives and children, Manólo's nephews and nieces.
His sister had married and her husband was gone too.

Manólo had always wondered what it meant to be
a Sereno. When he was twelve, with his friends Paco

26

Escobar, Estèfan Gutiérrez and other boys his age, they talked about it. But it was a subject that, like sex, seemed taboo. You didn't discuss it at home. It was taken for granted that, in time, you would find out, when you were old enough that is. Meanwhile Manólo and his two friends speculated about it. There weren't many in Cangas del Narcea who were literate but Pépé managed some written words once in a while and Manólo knew, from his father's letters, that it was an important job, in the BIG city, that you were given a huge ring to wear around your neck with many large keys on it.

How did you become a Sereno? Manólo didn't know and neither did his young friends. Some boys spoke with pretense of knowledge. It's an adventure. You have authority and respect. You have the keys. They are the keys of the city. The older boys laughed and said it was like going off to war. The young fathers always left as one might go off to do his duty for his country. The women stayed behind, brought up the children, ran the farms and shouldered each other in times of need.

Occasionally one of the men would return from the big city with an injury of some sort, a bad back or a limp, a little bit as if he were coming home wounded from the wars. The others stayed away for ten or twenty years and came back wrinkled and weather-beaten, squinting in daylight and opening their eyes wide, like cats, at night. Some didn't come back at all and Manólo and his friends assumed that they had died in battle.

The few who managed to write letters were proud and wanted the folks at home to be proud too, so they didn't write about the loneliness, the isolation and the monotony, nor about the cold and long winter nights. They wrote about the BIG city, and the responsibility, and all the important people they were "in contact with". So there was a myth in Cangas del Narcea about being a Sereno. The ones who returned were received by the town like heroes and the old ones, the gray ones, the wrinkled ones sat on their porch chairs or in the town saloon and talked about "the good old days" when they were "a Sereno in the big city". And they made up stories for Manólo and the boys, and embroidered, and glamorized, and perpetuated the myth.

*　　*　　*

WHEN HE WAS FOURTEEN Manólo left school and went to work in the mines. He had been a good student and even won a medal for being studious but the family was poor and they needed the additional income. He was a strapping young man, not tall but handsome and well built. With his friends Paco and Estèfan they would walk the path along the corn fields, swinging their lunch pails, laughing and ogling the girls bent over their chores between the corn stalks. And the girls would look up and chortle flirtatiously. "Hey Paco! Who's your friend?"

"The one you dream about" Paco would answer as Manólo straightened his miner's hat and looked away. Manólo was playful and boisterous at times but when it

28

came to girls he was shy and let Paco do the talking for him. On the other hand Paco was gregarious and enjoyed the exchange. He was tall and thin with a long neck which exaggerated his height. "I think some of these girls have a crush on you Manólo. Why don't you blow them a kiss and let them fight over which one it was meant for?" Manólo shrugged trying to hide his embarrassment.

"Leave him be!" Estèfan protested. "We're not all girl crazy like you".

Paco welcomed the challenge. He often kidded Estèfan. "I'll bet you haven't been kissed yet" Paco retorted.

"As often as you have chum" Estèfan shot back. "As often as you have". They walked on Paco and Estèfan nudging each other and laughing. But it was all in good fun. They were fast friends.

When they came to the mines it all stopped as the bright early morning sun disappeared over their heads in the elevator going down the mine shaft and everything was dark and the cave echoed with the noise of the axes swinging against the rock to loosen the coal. The air was thick with dust which filled their lungs. The boys worked in tandem, Estèfan and Manólo wielding the heavy edged cutting head vigorously against the rock and Paco loading the loosened coal into the carrier. They stopped frequently to wipe their forehead and the sweat stuck to the skin on the back of their necks. Like most miners they kept an eye on the canaries. There were several of them in cages throughout the shaft. They were a warning system for the miners. There was always the danger of a build-up of gases like methane and carbon monoxide, gases that have no color or odor and cannot not be detected but tend to lead to violent explosions. The canaries chirped and sang all day long. But if the carbon monoxide levels got too high the canaries would stop singing and the miners would know that the gas levels were dangerously high. They would leave the mine quickly to avoid being caught in an explosion.

When the foreman blew his whistle the noise ceased as the men laid down their axes and shovels and sat down to eat the lunch their women had prepared for them. The subterranean tunnel was like a bat cave illuminated throughout by the ever moving lights of the miners' hats. When they finished eating they washed down their gritty mouth with tepid cider and when the whistle blew again the men took up their tools and the noise resumed, filling each crevice of the battered shaft.

It was hard work but this is what they did. This is what everyone did and there was always the late afternoon Asturian sky above ground waiting for them. When the day's work was done and they came out of the mine you couldn't tell Manólo from Paco or Estèfan. The grime on their faces made them look like three ghosts from the underworld.

* * *

BEFORE GOING HOME they joined the miners at La Paloma, the local cider house where they took turns washing the day's coal dust off their hands and face before sitting around the long communal table or standing at the bar holding empty glasses, waiting. It was the season to tap the kegs of the new vintage of cider. A notable occasion. A time to celebrate.

Gigante, a bull of a man with the neck of a wrestler stood up. He had a shock of red hair and a ruddy complexion and could pass for an Irishman. "I think it's my turn!" he declared and looked around. The men nodded. Gigante picked up a tiny steel spigot from the shelf and walked over to the huge barrel against the far wall, scraped a tallow from a hole in a giant cider cask and inserted the spigot. All at once a thin stream of hard cider started to gush from the barrel. The men grabbed their glasses and rushed to the newly tapped barrel to catch a finger or two's worth of cider then headed back to the table. Paco, Estèfan, and Manólo filled their glasses as well, proud at fourteen to be men among men. There was a comradeship between the miners that was difficult to find elsewhere and it gave the boys a sense of togetherness, a sense of belonging which lightened the tiredness of the heavy day's work.

Marco, the host of the Sidrería, put platters of food on the long tables, mainly dried sausage and salt cod. The men reached over and helped themselves to the chorizo between rounds. The new vintage warranted a second helping, even a third, and during the course of the night several more barrels were tapped. As the evening wore on the men broke out in song which filled the cider house with warmth and merriment. Paco couldn't sing but Manólo had a good voice and joined in.

Marco brought out a few bottles of last year's cider. It had fermented a long time and was potent. He poured it from a height into a wide glass to get air bubbles into the drink giving it a sparkling taste like Champagne. Then he raised his glass shouting "Viva Asturias mi País" and the entire cider house shouted back in unison "Viva Asturias mi País".

As Paco couldn't carry a tune, he also couldn't hold his liquor. He stumbled across the Sidrería singing off key and slurring the words of "El mio Xuan". Later he was so far gone that he had to be carried home by Manólo and Estèfan. The moon was out and many men teetered along singing loud and strong into the night to relieve the tension of the day.

CHAPTER 4

IT WAS THE 18TH OF OCTOBER 1914 and it was Manólo's birthday. He was eighteen. He had contracted a deep asthma from the dust and given up the mines. He now worked in the fields with the horse and plow which let him be outdoors and be teased repeatedly by the girls. In a way, reserved as he was, he sort of enjoyed the teasing. It was the closest he had ever gotten to a girl.

Today was his birthday and the town was celebrating. When he was little his mother had told him that the celebration was in his honor. But it was Saint Teresa d'Avila, a religious feast for which the town was all decked out. The young women wore colorful folk costumes with lace fringes and black shawls over their heads. The older ones were all in black with large crosses hanging from their necks. Good Catholics one and all. All morning long a procession paraded an elaborately decorated statue of Saint Teresa d'Avila through the cobblestoned streets of the town to the church. There the town prayed with fervor for their husbands, sons and brothers who were Serenos in far away cities and they hadn't seen in many years. The atmosphere was stark and pious.

Then the sun went down and everything changed. The streets were lit up with brightly colored paper lanterns and everyone was outdoors, laughing and singing. On the main square some musicians were playing the gaita, the local bagpipe, a flute and a drum and, for lack of men, the women danced with each other or with young boys who buried their faces in their bosom. Manólo and Estèfan stood with a glass of wine by the long table, which had been set up and on which there was food and drink for all, when Paco came up with a girl.

"You remember Marie-Carmen don't you?" Manólo looked at her and their eyes met. She was a girl he knew long ago. They had played together when they were children but as they grew older the three year difference between them became a gap they could not cross and they lost contact with each other. And here she was, Marie-Carmen, a dark haired, dark eyed 15 year old beauty that he had known from childhood but this was their first real encounter.

"Hola!" she said and smiled. "Will you dance with me?". Her eyes glittered and she looked straight into his. "Will you dance with me?" she repeated. Manólo lowered his head. "I can't dance" he mumbled.

"I'll show you." she said and took him by the hand "Come!" and led him to the dance floor. Something clicked in Manólo as they danced the Muñeres to the gaita. It was a quick step number which resembled a jig. The Asturian Celts were first cousins to the Irish from when the Celts overran western Europe thousands of years ago and their music retained the Irish sound. It was lively and gay. The fast pace of the jig made it such that Manólo was lost and he just stood there and shuffled about while Marie-Carmen danced in front of him, her arms raised over her head and looked at him coyly. She was so full of life that Manólo struggled to keep his composure.

When the musicians played a slow piece, a number of older folks took to the floor. Manólo held Marie-Carmen at arms length but she pulled him in closer. He could feel and smell the sweet scent of her hair against his face and a gusher of love came bursting forth. His heart was pounding, his head was spinning, a feeling that went through his entire body right down to his fingers and the blood rushed to his face. Later he walked Marie-Carmen back to her house without holding hands or saying a word.

The next morning she invited him to come with her to Oviedo to visit her aunt Telma. She wore a lose blouse and a long flowing skirt and Manólo looked at her wide-eyed with admiration. She had packed a picnic basket to eat on the way. The bus was full of youths who were going to the sports stadium for the soccer match. Most of them didn't have a ticket but they snuck in by jumping a fence in back of the lockers. Manólo and Marie-Carmen sat in the last row and talked. Marie-Carmen had dropped out of school and was helping her mother and working with the girls in the field.

"I've seen you on the road with Paco and Estèfan on several occasions when you worked in the mines Manólo.

I was in the corn field when the girls teased you and you
needed Paco to speak up for you."

Manólo lowered his eyes. "Now I plow in the barley
and wheat fields on the far side of the Zolta farm and
there's a bunch of girls there too". Several boys turned
their heads, glared at them and chuckled. Marie-Carmen
tried to appear nonchalant. She took out some victuals
from her basket and they shared the food without saying
another word.

*   *   *

FEARING THAT THEIR EMOTIONS WOULD
SHOW they avoided each other for the next few days
but November first was All Saints' Day and Olivia,
Marie-Carmen's mother, invited Manólo for their
traditional family dinner.

As was the custom in Asturias, her brothers Sergio
and Vicente had slaughtered a pig for the occasion and it
was roasting on a spit in back of the house. They basted
it with pan drippings over and over again until it was a
golden brown and Olivia served it up with magostos the
local chestnuts. Manólo and Marie-Carmen looked at each
other dreamily from across the table. After the feast they
joined many others in the cemetery at the graves of their
loved ones which they adorned with beautiful flowers.
Marigolds were always in favor.

36

In the weeks that followed Manólo and Marie-Carmen were together as often as possible. They were comfortable with each other and Manólo broke through his shyness and found it easier to talk about himself, something he had never done, not even with his friends Paco and Estèfan. They often went down by the river bank and sat watching the barges loaded with coal that came by once in a while. There were restrained sparks on each occasion. The love between them was young and strong and gave their bodies a tingling sensation which was hard to resist and they fought vigorously against their natural instincts. They were Catholic as was the rest of the village and to yield to desire was a sin. They had to remain pure and Marie-Carmen had to remain a virgin. But the gusher was too strong and, despite their catholic upbringing, with feelings of guilt they gave way. They held hands and kissed and made love by the river.

For the next few months they met in secret and Manólo's emotions ran from guilt to love and back to guilt again, but he was happy, happier than he had ever been. Marie-Carmen gave him the locket of Saint Teresa that she wore around her neck and he gave her the medal of he had been awarded when he was twelve and under an Asturian sky filled with glittering stars they made vows to each other.

CHAPTER 5

IT WAS MID-AFTERNOON and the sun was still high when the postman came riding his bicycle through the fields, his cap jauntily on his head, his postman's satchel on a wide leather strap diagonally across his back. It was Santiago, the butcher who doubled as postman. On the rare occasion when a letter came, he would interrupt whatever he was doing, take off his white butcher's apron, don his official cap, hop on his bicycle and make the delivery. It wasn't often and, as he pedaled toward the farmhouse, the women in the fields raised their heads and followed him with their eyes.

As if she knew in advance, Amalia stood on the open porch in front of the house, her hands on her hips, waiting. She was a big woman. She had been a mother to five children and to many more not her own. The postman, out of breath, handed her the letter with a smile. Amalia took it. Proud and defiant she raised the unopened envelope over her head and looked out into the fields. And the women looked back and nodded. Then Amalia pulled the top of her blouse, stuffed the letter into her bosom, turned around and walked into the house. There's a letter. There's a letter from Pépé. It will be read tonight after dinner. Everyone will be there.

*   *   *

THE WOODEN TABLE WAS LONG and scratched with the markings of many years of use. Some twelve members of the family sat on benches on both sides and Amalia sat at the end and dished out the stew and the mashed potatoes as the plates were passed around. Manólo sat between Paco and Estèfan. There was not, as on other days, the loud banter and agitated conversation about the day's activities. All you could hear was the rattling of dishes and silverware as everyone more or less gulped down their food.

Before the meal was over several young men in miner's garb, with the lights still on their heads and their lunch pail in their hand, stood on the side waiting. The meal was over quicker than usual and all eyes became fixed on Amalia sitting at the head relishing the suspense. Slowly she reached into her blouse and pulled out the letter. She opened the envelope, unfolded the paper and looked at it intensely. Everyone was edgy and impatient. They all knew that Amalia didn't know how to read. Then she called "MANÓLO!" and handed the letter over to her son, a ritual that had gone on since Manólo was twelve. Everyone stretched their neck to hear as he read out loud the words of Pépé, the head of the family.

The letter told Amalia that Pépé was coming home. He had a bad fall and sustained a hip injury which did not allow him to stand for long periods of time. This made his job impossible. There was a mixture of sadness at Pépé's injury and excitement at his coming home on the train in the next few days. Manólo had not seen his father since he was two but, through the letters to his mother Amalia which he read diligently over the years, he had a great love and respect for him.

*   *   *

THE TRAIN STATION WAS ANCIENT and looked like an orphan abandoned in the middle of nowhere. There was an old bench and the wooden platform had broken planks. It was obvious that the train didn't stop there very often.

Amalia was dressed in her Sunday best. So was Manólo and his aunt Rosa. Pépé was coming home. Amalia had run the farm for sixteen years without the help of a man but he was the patriarch, the head of the family, if in name only. She was full of anticipation. It had been a long time since Amalia had seen Pépé. He was twenty-four when he left. Young and handsome she had enticed him into marriage.

At seventeen she was a big girl, attractive but plain and on the plump side. But she was mature for her age. She knew the limits of her attractiveness. Young men would often tease her older sister Rosa sing-songing:

> *"Twenty-one, twenty one,*
> *getting on at twenty-one.*
> *No suitor, no young man,*
> *soon enough you'll be a nun".*

Amalia was determined she would not be the butt of their derision. Pépé was her cousin. He was tall, good-looking and naive and she put her mark on him. She went about it deliberately. She offered him her big bosom and allowed herself to be seduced. As it would happen she became pregnant knowing that Pépé would "do the right thing" by her and he did. He married her. He had been ensnared by her wiles but she turned out to be a good woman and he grew to care for her and was thankful for her warmth, the strength of her character and the size of her breasts.

She wanted to run a household and have children. And children she had. Five of them. One after the other. They ran all over the house and Amalia would call them to order. Her sister Rosa lived with them and Amalia ordered her around too. She was somewhat bossy. She would justify her bossiness by saying "I'm the one who kills the chicken and plucks the feathers". But she was a real mama and everyone loved her.

Not to think that Pépé was spared. He often wandered off into the fields to avoid her cackling. So when he was called to be a Sereno there was a sense of loss but also of relief. Still, in Madrid in the evenings before going on duty, he would sit at the table in his sparsely furnished room and write letters to his family by the light of a candle, maintaining his status from afar.

Amalia flinched when the whistle of the locomotive blew and the train pulled in and came to a screeching stop.

From the last car came Pépé limping slightly and leaning on his cane. He was taller and better looking than she had remembered him to be. The years had given his good looks a handsome maturity. On the other hand Amalia wasn't plump anymore. She had presence and stature. She looked better to him than when he left. There was a lot of emotion at this family reunion but it was never expressed openly. Just a slap on the back, an embrace and a kiss on each cheek as the train disappeared in the distance.

* * *

IN THE EVENING, after dinner, many of the villagers came to welcome Pépé back. Among them were old-timers who looked forward to hearing about the streets of the barrios of Madrid where long ago they had walked the night with the heavy ring of keys around their neck. There was much drinking and excited conversation and it was nearly two o'clock when the last of them left.

Amalia had not had a man in her bed in a long time and all her feistiness vanished in front of the prospect and she trembled like a young girl as she laid down next to him and blew out the candle. That first night she became aware of how much she had missed the intimacy and welcomed his advances as she welcomed him home.

In the morning Pépé took Manólo to his room. He sat in the old armchair by the window and had him stand rigidly in front of him. He looked him over from head to toe not saying a word for a weighty moment. Then he rubbed his chin. "I know you're only nineteen but your time has come" he announced. "You must go to Madrid and be the Sereno in my place. I have gotten a temporary replacement but only for one week. So you will leave tomorrow." That was it. There was nothing to do. Like a good soldier Manólo had received his orders.

With a slight show of emotion Pépé took out his pocket watch, wound it slowly and looked up at Manólo. "Here! You will find that time takes on a different dimension when you're a Sereno" he said handing him the watch, "it stretches out into the night when the street lamps go on and becomes immeasurable until dawn turns them off again". Manólo didn't quite understand what Pépé meant but he nodded. Then Pépé took the chuzo he had gotten from his father many years ago, a cane that was sturdy and made of madrone. It had been in the family for many generations. On the knob was a handcarved bull's head which was worn down by the many hands that had held it. With great ceremony Pépé handed the cane over to Manólo and looked at him with pride. Manólo felt his father's pocket watch in one hand and the knob of the chuzo in the palm of the other and a shiver went down his back.

That night Manólo was too excited to sleep. This was the big adventure he had been looking forward to for a long time and it came on so suddenly and unexpectedly. He was not prepared for it. He thought he had several years yet before he would take over his father's mantle. His thoughts raced through his mind wild and wondrous and came to an abrupt halt at Marie-Carmen. In his excitement he had not thought of her and his elation turned to distress at the impending separation for what would probably be a long time. He tossed and turned and tried to make peace with the inevitable but his heart ached and sleep came with great difficulty.

* * *

IN THE MORNING Amalia packed a small cardboard suitcase tied with string, a bundle with food to eat on the train, and the family and almost the entire village accompanied Manólo to the station. It was a send off they had known many times before. Paco and Estèfan walked arm in arm with Manólo, fully aware that it would be a long time before they would see each other again. On the platform, waiting for the train, Manólo was hugged and slapped on the back and each time he looked over the shoulder of the person hugging him he saw Marie-Carmen standing on the side sorrowfully sad but resolved. At the last he could not take her in his arms or give her the kind of embrace that would show his love because their relationship had remained a secret and it could not surface now. So with the waving handkerchiefs of his well-wishers and a sad farewell to Paco, Estèfan and to his beloved Marie-Carmen, Manólo took the train to the unknown, somewhere in a barrio of Madrid.

CHAPTER 6

WITH THE TRAIN CHUG CHUGGING AWAY, plumes of smoke billowing from the locomotive and long stops for coal, it took almost twenty four hours from Cangas to Madrid, much time to look, to think, to dream. There were only two passengers in Manólo's compartment, a genteel looking woman in her thirties and her 12 year old son. They exchanged politeness and Manólo settled in by the window. He was excited. The ride was exhilarating. He had never seen such diverse landscapes. There were vineyards and almond trees in bloom, and groves of olive trees, with an occasional windmill. Manólo loved the land. He was proud to be an Asturian. The countryside was beautiful. The air was fresh and clean and the sky was bright and so near you could almost touch it. Red poppies all over the landscape.

The train bumped along at such a slow pace that Manólo could count the cows in the fields then a large farm with a barn and a milkmaid carrying a bucket. Marie-Carmen came to his mind and a burst of love filled him with longing. Would he see her again? If he had stayed in Cangas del Narcea he would have married her and started a family but he was called to duty before that could happen and now he was left wondering. He was also wondering at what lay ahead of him. All the fantasies that he had built up over the years about being a Sereno had led him to expectations and it would all come to pass at the end of this train ride. He looked at the woman and her son. If they only knew that he was going to Madrid to be a "Sereno" he thought. They might from the chuzo he was holding. The thought made him smile and the woman smiled back.

The chug chug of the train had a soothing rhythm and Manólo looked so intensely out the window that his eyes became blurry and he dozed off. He went in and out of dreams filled with light and the brightness of the sky over Cangas del Narcea, with Marie-Carmen lying on the grass by the river, with tales of the big city that he had heard over the years. He slept a long time. The siren of the locomotive startled him awake and the smoke flashed in front of the window. Suddenly seized by the fear of the unknown he reached for the bastion his father had given him. It had strength, gave him comfort and he held it tight.

*   *   *

IN THE BARRIO cousin José had filled in for Pépé. He was short and stocky and was missing three fingers on his right hand from a mining accident he had before he left Asturias for Madrid. In back of the courtyard of an abandoned and dilapidated compound José had his living quarters. It consisted of a room with a metal framed bed and a broken lighting fixture hanging from the ceiling.

Next to it was a kitchen with a wood stove, a table and two wooden chairs.

He set Manólo up on a cot and tried to make him as comfortable as he could. Then he took a bottle of Sidra and two glasses from the cupboard and poured one for himself and Manólo. "This is all I've got left of Asturias" he said with nostalgia, "memories in a glass of Sidra". He shook his head and raised the glass for Manólo to clink. It was a picture like a van Gogh painting. José the older man slightly bent over and worn at the edges and Manólo, barely nineteen, bright-eyed and fresh from the lush green countryside. The two of them, more than a generation apart, across from each other, with a shaded lamp hanging low over the table.

Then José leaned back and asked. He wanted to know everything and anything Manólo could tell him about Cangas del Narcea, about the family, the old ones, the young ones, the fields and the farms. He hadn't been back in many years. He wanted details and closed his eyes dreamily.

When he was satisfied with Manólo's telling he took out the ring of keys and set them on the table. They were large keys and José had Manólo finger each one to notice the feel, the weight, and the contour with a critical examination. At noon he undressed and went to bed. Manólo wasn't used to going to bed in the daytime but then again he wasn't used to being up all night either.

* * *

FOR A WEEK JOSÉ TOOK MANÓLO around from house to house, from street to street, and showed him the ropes. He gave him the ring with nearly seventy keys on it, arranged from large to small. He told him that on some level he was an officer of the law and was responsible for maintaining order. Manólo straightened up taking pride in the designation. José also gave him a whistle to use if needed to call other Serenos to help.

The barrio was a middle class barrio with well to do families living alongside more modest ones on the far end. It was clustered around the Plaza San Ramón where stood the Iglesia de la Madonna an eleventh century church whose bells rang on Sundays to call the faithful to Mass. There were a number of Cafés on opposite sides of the square, a bar which was always noisy, and a row of stores in between, a butcher shop, a baker, a tailor, and a general store with hardware, candles, barrels of grain and coffee. The Sereno did not have the keys to these stores but it was his job to check that they were properly locked every night.

In time Manólo would find out that the baker Señor Valparo started his ovens at three in the morning and baked his breads all night. José told Manólo that on cold nights he often spent part of the night near there because of the warmth of the ovens and the sweet smell of the breads that wafted out from the transom into the street. In the middle of the square there were benches where old men

49

played checkers in the daytime and lovers held hands and embraced when night fell.

When the week was up José went back to his own barrio leaving Manólo to walk the deserted streets waiting to be called by a clap clap somewhere. He arranged his lodgings as best he could. From his suitcase he took out a pen and ink drawing of Marie-Carmen, which had been done by a roving artist last spring, and put it on the night table. At noon he undressed and went to bed. It felt strange and he had a time falling asleep, waking up now and then from the noise of children playing in the courtyard.

When night came he checked his watch and at ten o'clock he donned his smock, put the ring of keys around his neck and went out into the street. The habit of Spaniards to eat supper at eleven kept Manólo busy till well past two and the claps seem to come from everywhere. He hadn't yet learned the ways of what would become his flock so he ran the length of the barrio many times over, keeping the residents waiting in front of their portal. But he was young and they appreciated his effort and his youth and the tips were generous and given with a smile. Yet no one asked his name. It was as if he hadn't any.

As the night wore on things calmed down. An occasional night reveler broke the silence and called him to duty. Then all was quiet, so quiet he could hear his own steps on the cobblestoned pavement. The silence was heavy and was the most difficult thing he had to get used to. The only thing that broke the stillness was a cough from a window somewhere or the shrieks of a cat fight in the back of an alley.

Manólo realized that being a Sereno was not what he had imagined it to be. He was only nineteen and had expected something that would live up to the fantasy he had built up in his mind, something that would help him forget Marie-Carmen but this wasn't it. It was a menial job, an anonymous job, a lonely job. From living under the bright sky of Asturias he now lived in the somber night of Madrid.

*   *   *

IT WASN'T LONG before Manólo got to know all the people who lived in his barrio. He didn't know them personally but he knew who they were, what they did, and many of the details of their lives.

There was the Contessa de las Torres who lived in luxury behind a beautifully ornate portal on the south side of the street and enjoyed flirting with the young Sereno. It brought back her own youth and she rewarded him with a silver coin on occasion.

There was Carlos and Gisella and their two children. He knew they had children even though he never saw them. He knew because he heard them cry at different times of night for an ache or a pain and call out a tearful "Mama" which could be heard from the street.

There was also Pedro Valdez, a middle-aged Madrilleno who had been a matador in his day, celebrated as "El Honcho", and gored by the last bull he fought in the arena. Now on crutches, he lived in isolation over the bar and spent much of his time downstairs, drinking and reading about the last Sunday's corrida to remind himself of the days when he held the red cape and waved it in front of the charging bull.

At the far end of the barrio the silence was broken by the noise of music, the sound of laughter and song coming from bars and cafés that remained open late to accommodate the fun loving night frolickers who made merry till all hours of the morning. Manólo liked to spend some of his time close by. He knew the noise echoed through the streets and disturbed some of the residents but they were used to it and he found it indulgent to let them have their fun. It was strange. He was overseeing the activities of an adult community. Here he was, an adolescent, and it was up to him to be "indulgent" and "let them have their fun". He shrugged it off. He had vicarious pleasure in their merriment.

Not far off, tucked away in an alley, there was a house of ill repute. Its door was open all the time. One did not clap clap in front of that door. One simply struck the brass knocker and would be admitted without question. It was run by a lady they called La Gorda and when business was slow she sent some of the girls into darkened doorways to wait for their prey.

When the cafés closed the revelers spilled out into the street and fanned out in all directions. Some of them sauntered leisurely arm in arm singing loudly the last refrain. Others were waylaid by one of La Gorda's ladies of the night for a quick romp before finding their way home.

*   *   *

IT WAS A COLD NIGHT and Manólo wrapped the shawl tightly around his neck. He had answered the last of his pressing calls and "tucked his flock into bed". Now he was alone with himself and the night. He walked counting the steps as he had counted the telephone poles out the window of the train on his train ride from Asturias.

A hacking cough stirred him from his thoughts and brought him back to alertness. It came from a darkened doorway and Manólo approached it with caution keeping his chuzo tightly in hand. A dark figure was curled up against the wall covered with newspapers as protection against the cold. The man had been sleeping and the wracking cough had brought him out of his slumber.

Upon seeing the Sereno he rose quickly and drew back. "No soy un ladrón. I am not a thief Señor" he muttered in fear. Manólo took him by the arm and led him into the light of the lamp post. He was thin. His face was drawn and his clothes were shabby. But underneath this façade there was the glimmer of a has-been who had fallen on hard times.

Manólo felt sorry for him. "Are you hungry?" he asked. The man nodded. "Venga!" Manólo said and walked him to his quarters. The stove was still warm and he stirred it and added a log. He took some bread and cheese out of the cupboard and a bottle of wine and set it on the table. The man stood wide-eyed.

"My name is . . ."

"It doesn't matter" Manólo interrupted. "You eat then you can rest on the cot till morning. I'll be back after my shift" and walked back out onto the street.

The rest of the night felt good to Manólo and he didn't feel the cold as he had before. When he returned to his quarters in the morning the man was gone. On the table was a note. "Gracias Señor. My name is Angel. May God bless you".

⌒⌒•⌒⌒

CHAPTER 7

THE CLAP CLAP WAS FAMILIAR and expected. Manólo looked at his watch. Three thirty. There were very few clap claps at that hour of the night. He knew where it came from and who it was. For some time now he had opened the portal for him at a very late hour. The first time he answered the call he found a handsome young man waiting under the lamp post. He was taller and somewhat younger than Manólo. He wore a black cape and the orange scarf of the students of the Academy. He was impressive. Manólo stepped out of the darkness and they exchanged glances under the street light when Manólo searched for the keys. His was the soft and intelligent face of a philosopher, an intellectual. There was no mistaking it. Just as there was no mistaking that Manólo, with his square features and his pallid eyes, was of peasant stock.

"Miguel Arroyo" he said looking Manólo straight in the eyes. Manólo avoided his look. "And you?" In his first few weeks in the barrio Manólo had received a tip and a nod from the residents but no one had ever posed the question. "And you?" Miguel repeated.

"Manólo" he answered.

Miguel nodded and handed him a coin. "Buenas noches Manólo" he said as he went in and closed the

55

portal behind him. Manólo straightened up and raised his head. Miguel Arroyo had called him by name. He had acknowledged his identity.

In the weeks that followed Manólo answered Miguel's clap on many occasions and there was never more than an exchange of greetings between them but there was warmth in the exchange. There was also something in Miguel's demeanor that puzzled Manólo. His coming and goings seemed timed and, although he left with a bundle under his cape, he always came back empty handed.

* * *

IT WAS 1915 AND WORLD WAR I WAS RAGING but Spain remained neutral. Still the Spanish were divided between the Aliadofilos, liberals, intellectuals, republicans and workers, who sided with the allies, and the Germanofilos, the clergy, the army, government officials and business people, all entrenched groups. Among the adults you couldn't tell who was an Aliadofilo and who a Germanofilo. But at the University the students were thrown together, sons of the rich and sons of the populists and they had frequent encounters with each other. The increasing hostility created by this unrest resulted in major workers' strikes which were put down by the army, an army of less than 50,000 soldiers led by a privileged class of 500 generals and 4,000 career officers who looked down upon the working class and had no qualms about ordering the use of maximum force to bring the strikers into line.

*   *   *

Madrid
June 21, 1915

Querida Marie-Carmen,

It feels as though I've left you ages ago. So many things have taken place and you're so far away. I am now "a Sereno". I am in charge of a whole neighborhood and have the respect of the entire community.

I've met a young man from the Academy. His name is Miguel Arroyo. He's 17 and lives with his parents. If he were with me in Asturias we might have been friends but he is educated and I am not.

I am making good money and will soon be sending some to Mama. I miss the sky over Asturias and the wide open fields and above all I miss you. If I had wings I'd fly into your arms but the train is so slow that I don't know when I'll see you again. I am not good with words but I hold you in my heart and send you my love.

Manólo

*   *   *

ON THE NORTH END OF THE BARRIO there was a small plaza with two globe shaped gas lamps that sprayed a yellow light up the treetops, and several benches where couples on a romantic night stroll ended up in an embrace and a kiss under the trees. Manólo made it a point to avoid going through the square so as not to disturb the lovers. On occasion, however, he noticed Miguel Arroyo and several young men his age huddling surreptitiously near one of the benches. Their faces were tense and they looked around uneasily. Manólo was sure they were up to something and it wasn't a prank on some fellow student or a fraternity hazing. They were plotting something but Manólo couldn't figure out what.

One evening around 11 PM Miguel came out of his compound and clapped in front of his open portal. When Manólo arrived Miguel told him he was expecting some "friends" and instructed Manólo to let them in. Manólo knew who lived where and he wasn't about to open the door for a stranger unless he was told to. Over the next few hours they came, separately or in twos. Some wore the cape and orange scarf but others wore work clothes and heavy shoes. It was a strange mix of young people. Manólo suspected Miguel was involved in some clandestine activities probably working with the Aliadofilos, posting opposition on the walls and placing tracts on café tables. What's more Miguel knew of Manólo's suspicions and it created a complicity which never surfaced but there was a silent kinship which developed between them and grew stronger with time. Manólo liked Miguel and it got him interested in the politics of the day.

*   *   *

ALEXANDER ARROYO, Miguel's father was tall and lanky, a man of poise and stature. He was a doctor and made house calls though hardly ever at night. So when, in response to a clap clap, Manólo found him at one o'clock in the morning standing in front of the portal with his physician's satchel in hand he bowed to him with reverence as he fumbled for the key.

"You are Manólo?" he asked.

"Yes sir, I am".

Doctor Arroyo nodded approvingly. "Miguel has spoken of you".

"I hope I haven't offended him in some way".

"No! Not at all." Dr. Arroyo started to go in then turned around and looked at Manólo. "You are very young. Our last Sereno was someone much older than you. Are you related to him?"

"He is my father".

"Oh! He was a fine man. I treated him when he broke his hip. He took a big fall and I'm afraid he'll never be able to walk without a cane. How is your father these days?"

"He is well. Thank you for asking".

"That's good. Buenas noches".

"Buenas noches Doctor Arroyo". And the portal closed behind him. Manólo was elated. This was a real conversation, not only with one of his residents, but with the father of someone he esteemed.

On market day he had seen Miguel and his mother shopping for vegetables at the open stalls. Her hair was tied in a bun and framed a face that was warm and friendly. Miguel clumsily juggled the many shopping bags and nearly dropped one when he spotted Manólo and tried to wave at him. Manólo couldn't help but laugh and a remnant of their mutual adolescence surfaced momentarily.

But Miguel was a man at seventeen and seriously engaged in political doings that his father knew about but pretended not to. The tracts that he put out were done on a mimeograph machine in the cellar of a fellow student of the Academy named Cortez. There was also Adolfo and Simon and they were united in their mutual concerns. When they didn't study or make music together they took pleasure in their surreptitious extracurricular activities, a cause, the manifestation of a youthful idealism.

CHAPTER 8

MARIE-CARMEN WOKE UP feeling nauseous. She had missed her period for two months and the morning sickness confirmed her worst misgivings. She didn't know what to do or who to turn to. Olivia, her mother, was a pious Catholic and the pregnancy would destroy her. Her two older brothers would not understand. How could she have allowed this to happen? The fear that gripped her kept her up at night and she cried softly into her pillow.

Words were whispered when she began to show and many villagers snubbed her and looked the other way when she passed. Her mother stopped speaking to her and wore her shame like a shawl around her neck. But Amalia, Manólo's mama, took to Marie-Carmen and held her against her bosom. She had gone through the same thing herself and knew her son would "do the right thing" as Pépé had done with her. She persuaded Marie-Carmen to overcome her reluctance and write to Manólo.

Cangas del Narcea
July 11, 1915

Querida Manólo,
It is a difficult letter I have to write to you. I have some news that you may not welcome . . .

Manólo was taken aback but he was overjoyed. He recalled the night they made vows to each other, a solemn promise which Manólo's premature call to duty in Madrid had prevented fulfillment. Now providence had intervened. It was as if God had taken over and decided what was to be. Manólo was jubilant and looking forward to taking Marie-Carmen in his arms and welcoming the unexpected birth. He talked to José and managed to get someone to fill in for him so he could go back to Cangas del Narcea for a spell.

* * *

ON THE LONG TRAIN RIDE BACK Manólo looked wide-eyed at the Asturian landscape. It had only been a few months since he left but he saw it as if for the first time. The Madrid nights had closed him in. In contrast with the narrow streets of his barrio there was such a vast expanse of space, such a broad horizon, such a transcendent sky that it made him light-headed. He thought of Marie-Carmen and pictured her with love in his mind. He never thought this would come about and was awed by the miracle of it. Suddenly he realized the shame and humiliation Marie-Carmen must have endured. It's not that he was insensitive but Manólo was so overwhelmingly happy that it had blotted out everything else. Now he saw it as it probably was, people sneering, expressing scorn and contempt, pointing fingers and whispering under their breaths.

When the train pulled in at the station she was alone on the platform. She looked so small and vulnerable. He rushed to her and took her in his arms. *"Oh! Marie-Carmen what an ordeal you must have gone through."* Marie-Carmen took his hand and put it on her breast and he felt her heart as he felt his own beating rapidly. Then he pressed up against her swollen belly and felt the life in her womb, the child he had sired. He looked around. There was no one on the platform. He reached over and kissed her tenderly.

Manólo's mother had stayed in the horse and wagon to give the lovers a time to themselves. Now she appeared on the path and Manólo put his arm around Marie-Carmen and they walked toward her. Amalia took both their hands and smiled at them benevolently. *"You look good together. It will be a great day. There's a whole town waiting for you."*

*   *   *

OLIVIA, MARIE-CARMEN'S MOTHER, had published the wedding banns in anticipation, not so much as an announcement of matrimony but as a declaration to the townsfolk that all would be made right. And on a warm Sunday in July Manólo took Marie-Carmen to the altar. The pregnant bride was escorted to the church by the scornful villagers. It wasn't a ceremonial procession. It was a purposeful march to repair a broken commandment. The bride was not dressed in white. White indicated purity and innocence and her condition showed otherwise. She wore a silver gray dress and her dark eyes and olive complexion radiated happiness in the midst of the scorn all around her. But she wouldn't let herself be brought down on this momentous day in her young life.

She came down the hill accompanied by her mother and a number of town spinsters who had cackled viciously in the preceding months. Manólo stood in front of the church with Amalia wearing the dress of white lace she had worn at her own wedding so long ago and Pépé wearing his Sunday suit and leaning on his cane.

When Marie-Carmen walked up the steps of the church Manólo took her hand and she smiled. It was the same smile that had seduced him when he met her at the dance on Saint Teresa d'Avila. They walked down the isle together and stood by the altar in front of Father Antonio Canteras who had known them since birth and baptized them. Paco and Estèfan stood cardboard stiff in the first row. A beam of light from a single stained glass window depicting the Virgin Mary and the Christ child shone down upon the couple as they made their vows. The ceremony was short and Father Canteras called the Lord's blessing down upon them. This was followed by a collective sigh of relief. The lone soprano voice of a twelve year old choir boy singing Ave Maria floated above them as they walked out into the sunlight and it was as if Manólo and Marie-Carmen had been cleansed and there was forgiveness and rejoicing and much drinking and dancing for two days and nights.

Then Manólo returned to Madrid.

* * *

"WHERE WERE YOU? Miguel asked Manólo under the street lamp. "When we saw José doing your job we thought we had lost you." The question was so sincere and full of concern that Manólo had to respond.

"I . . . I got married. I went back to Asturias and got married." Suddenly Manólo felt the need to shout his happiness out loud. "And I'm going to be a father. And her name is Marie-Carmen. And she's beautiful." Then Manólo quickly ducked into the shadow and disappeared.

The next few months went by fast. He played games with the cobblestones as one might with the petals of a daisy saying "She loves me. She loves me not." But it was "It's a boy. It's a girl. It's a boy. It's a girl." Boy or girl it didn't matter to Manólo. He was full of joy. To help pass the time he had begun to read.

Miguel came home one evening carrying a stack of books. When one of them fell Manólo picked it up and looked at it before handing it back to Miguel.

"Can you read Manólo?"

"Yes".

"Then take it!"

Manólo hesitated but the look in Miguel's eyes could not be denied so he took the book and put it under his arm. No tip could ever match the gift of a book.

CHAPTER 9

ON SUNDAY MORNING at eleven there was a Tertulia, a gathering of poets at La Pluma on the Plaza San Ramón. They came early and sat around and talked. There was the Spanish modernist Francisco Villaespesa, and the Nicaraguan Rubén Darío. Darío was 48, but he had displayed such talent from an early age that he gained a reputation as 'El Niño Poeta' the poet child, a moniker he had tried to live up to ever since. Both of them had been invited by Juan Ramón Jiménez Madrid's resident poet. There was also Federico García Lorca who, at 17, was an emerging light in the world of poetry. Villaespesa was cocky. "I write" he said pretentiously "to lyrically magnify the spirit of Granada". This resonated with García Lorca who came from Fuente Vaqueros, a village on the banks of the River Genil, a few miles from Granada. These were the literati whose names were only beginning to be recognized. García Lorca was by far the youngest but he was the center of attraction.

At la Puerta del Sol, on the other side of the square, many Serenos came together for a vaso de vino before heading for Mass. At their gathering Manólo, the youngest, was also the center of attraction. Most of them were much older or at least they seemed so. Perhaps the darkness had aged them somewhat. The old timers patted him on the back. He was the new lad in town. They never thought of asking him how he was doing. Instead they all pumped him with questions about Asturias and he found himself repeating the stories he had told José. They listened attentively, wide eyed and breathing in deeply as if to catch a breath of the air of Cangas del Narcea coming from this recent arrival.

Then the church bells rang and it was time for mass at the Iglesia de la Madonna. The poets remained at the Tertulia philosophizing about the existence of God but the Serenos had no doubts that Jesus awaited their confession.

Manólo sat in one of the pews in the back listening to the organ music and clutching the locket of Saint Teresa d'Avila that Marie-Carmen had given him on his eighteenth birthday. He closed his eyes and thanked Saint Teresa for his happiness.

When Father Antonio Suarez started his sermon Manólo spotted Miguel Arroyo with his parents in the third row. He was sitting stiffly and it was clear he was uncomfortable. He was there because his parents were there and when the priest made allusions to the Kaiser and the German folk Manólo could see Miguel flinch. He was politically ignorant but his regard for Miguel made him sympathize with his cause whatever that might be.

*　*　*

MANÓLO WAS HAPPY. Nothing could bother him. He read a lot, mostly romantic novels which helped him pass the months of impatience and anticipation. There was so much joy to look forward to. He drank it in and it made him almost tipsy. Even though he knew the distance between Madrid and Cangas del Narcea was so great that he would not get to see his bride or the baby more than every few years, it made a bridge between them, between Cangas and Madrid. Every once in a while he would daydream of bringing her and the baby to the city and setting them up in an apartment together. He knew this was impossible but the daydream made him happy.

A fight between two drunks, a squabble between a husband and wife which seem to happen pretty often, the time when two of the lamp lights were broken and he filled his pocket with small candles which he lit and gave the house dwellers to find their way up the darkened staircase, it was all part of the job and kept him busy.

He had a calendar next to his bed and every night he marked off another day. October and November went by . . . then it came. It came in the mail like a sledge hammer, a letter that would shatter the dream and crush him. It was a letter from his friend Paco in Asturias. The envelope had a black border signifying a death announcement and it sent a shudder through his body. He saw his father's face flash briefly in front of him and had an immediate sense of loss. He opened the envelope slowly and took out the paper.

Dear Manólo,

*I have some sad news for you. There's
been a tragedy and I know it will be a shock.
Marie-Carmen and the baby died in childbirth.
The midwife did everything she could to save
her. Amalia was with her at the end. Her last
words were for you.*

*I don't know what to say to comfort you
my friend. Everyone sends you their sympathy.
She was a beautiful lady. May she rest in
peace. Que vaya con Dios mi amigo!*

Paco

P.S. It was a boy.

Manólo fell to the floor and let out a scream that could
be heard throughout the barrio. He sobbed uncontrollably
unable to suppress his grief. *"WHY? DEAR GOD, WHY?"*
He picked up the letter and read it again through his tears
hoping he had read it wrong the first time but he hadn't.
Life had dealt him a heavy blow and he was devastated. He
didn't even go back for the funeral. A widower at twenty
he was inconsolable and he knew he would never marry
again. For him the night had become his shroud.

He sowed a black armband on the sleeve of his coat
and carried the grief with him in the locket that hung
around his neck. The nights were long and empty and

drawn out. His dreams were filled with sunsets over Cangas del Narcea where Marle-Carmen's face was the face of the sun disappearing over the horizon and dusk set in leaving the Asturian sky in total darkness. The loss was immeasurable, gut wrenching. It was as if his sorrow had turned him into a child and he retreated into his barrio like a child hiding in a closet. It became his world and he remained a shadow, an anonymous identity, a nobody.

CHAPTER 10

WHEN MIGUEL FOUND OUT the cause of Manólo's despondency there was a tremendous amount of compassion. He put his arms around him and invited him in for a drink but Manólo would not drink while he was on duty. So they met in the afternoon on the terrace of the Café Nueva Roma. It was the first time they sat together in the daylight, two young men older than their age, the one because of his beliefs, the other because of his grief. The café was crowded and they sat at a sidewalk table drinking a cortado.

Miguel put his hand on Manólo's shoulder and tried to get him to open up and speak about his loss but much as he tried Manólo remained quiet. The grief was heavy but could not be shared. They sat in silence.

All of a sudden a brouhaha erupted across the street. Words had been exchanged between two factory workers who were passing by and some business men sitting at a table drinking their cognac and it wound up in an exchange of blows. Fists were thrown and tables and chairs were knocked over. The whole café stood aside fearful of getting embroiled. The owner called the police. Within minutes a siren whistled and a police van pulled up to the curb. Eight uniformed police officers wielded their clubs and broke up the fight. Without seeking to find out who the culprits were the officer in charge ordered the arrest of the workmen. They used their clubs mercilessly and dragged them to their paddy wagon. Miguel stood up and winced then sat down angrily.

In a quick thought he decided to take Manólo's mind off his loss by confiding in him the activities he was engaged in and trying to enlist him to the cause. It wasn't an extreme cause because the government wasn't the object. It was simply an effort to redirect the upper class Spaniards' views and change public opinion to side with the Allies and not the Germans in the war that was raging in France and causing so many casualties. Manólo wasn't surprised by the revelation. He had suspected something all along. He was deeply moved by the invitation and the trust it implied and accepted readily.

The next day Miguel took him to the hideout and introduced him to Cortez, Adolfo and Simón. They were all about the same age, students of the Academy but each had a flair of his own. Cortez was the poet of the group. It was mostly he who wrote the tracts. Many of them were in the form of poetry. Adolpho was the technician. It was his mimeograph machine. He had borrowed it from his father under false pretense and hand carried the heavy machine from some twenty cuadras away. Simón was not an idealist like Miguel. He was in it for the fun and the thrill. He had no real convictions but they all worked well together and took Manólo in without question.

For the next twelve months Manólo spent his days leaving tracts on café tables and slipping them under doorways at night. It kept him busy and gave him a sense of purpose. It also allowed time to go by and numb him from the pain of his bereavement. Something else happened during this time. A silent friendship developed between him and Miguel, a friendship that overcame the difference between them.

*　　*　　*

THERE WERE OTHER SOURCES of comfort for Manólo. The ladies of the night were among the few who knew him by name. La Gorda, the Madam, had short flaming red hair and the warmth of a Mama and she teased him every so often. She introduced Manólo to Gabriella de Flores who had come to work for her.

Gabriella was from Rinconcillo, a town on the southern coast of Spain near Gibraltar. Her father Heraldo, who had been a tradesman, died of tuberculosis when she was only five. Bertha, her English mother, was a grieving widow for several years and tried to manage with the dwindling money her husband had left her. When Colón, the owner of the local café who also ran a gambling room in back of the bar, began courting her she cast emotions aside and looked at him as a security blanket to provide for herself and her daughter. She had queasy feelings about him because of his coarse demeanor but she ignored the warnings. She thought of herself as secondhand merchandise and when he offered her a ring she accepted it. They were married at City Hall and there was no reception or wedding party.

After the marriage Colón moved Bertha and Gabriella to an apartment over the bar. He came home late, after a night of drinking and gambling and forced himself upon his wife while she was sleeping.

There was a nineteen year old young woman named Marisol who cleaned up after the patrons left and the bar closed. She slept in a small room behind the kitchen and became Colón's toy. He molested her and she suffered greatly from his violent sexual advances. She had been a novitiate and left the convent before the marriage to Christ. She tolerated Colón because between bouts he gave her money, because her family had renounced her for leaving the convent, and because she had no where to go.

When Gabriella was seven she wandered into Marisol's room for a reason she does not recall. She opened the door of her closet and was stunned by Marisol's gray habit, the large cross on a heavy chain and Jesus painfully crucified. To small petrified Gabriella the image of the bleeding Christ would remain forever imprinted on her mind and become the subject of often recurring dreams from which she would wake up screaming. One day Marisol was gone. Did she finally get the courage to reject Colón's brutalizing her? Did she become pregnant and Colón threw her out? The reason was never clear. Bertha knew all this but decided to live with it. As long as Colón had Marisol to abuse he left her more or less alone.

Several months after Marisol vanished Colón became violent. His outbursts often ended with striking Bertha across the face, sometimes sending her to the hospital. One day, when Bertha was out and Gabriella was ten and alone in her room, Colón came in and unzipped his pants. Gabriella froze and as he came toward her she screamed. Colón put his hand over her mouth and nailed her against the wall. "You scream again and I'll beat you to a pulp you hear?" Then he threw her on the bed and forced himself into her while she cried hysterically. It didn't take long but to Gabriella it was an eternity and when he left, the sheets were bloody and her crotch was torn. This scene repeated itself over and over again with Colón's admonition "you tell anyone about this and I'll kill you and your mother". Though Gabriella never did, for fear of her stepfather, she was sure her mother Bertha knew and looked the other way.

For several years this child rape continued unabated and Gabriella lived in constant fear whenever she was in her room and heard her stepfather's footsteps. When she turned fourteen Gabriella took it upon herself to take charge of her life. She went into the bar in the early morning hours when Colón was still sleeping and the chairs were stacked on the tables, opened the cash register behind the counter and took all the money. Then she packed a small suitcase and fled the scene of her torment. She hopped a train to Madrid trying to put a great distance between her and the horrors she had endured for so long.

At fourteen Gabriella was only a child but her experiences had been painful and made her grow up quickly. She found herself in Madrid and the little money she had ran out fast. She wound up sleeping in doorways and eating out of garbage cans.

One evening, as she was rummaging through the leavings by the backdoor of a restaurant, a woman stopped her. "What are you doing child? she asked. Gabriella did not respond. She looked left and right and prepared to run. "Don't be frightened child. Are you hungry?" The woman didn't wait for an answer. She took her by the hand and walked her to the corner. "They call me La Gorda. What's your name?"

"Gabriella."

Where are you from Gabriella?" Gabriella stood silent. She was afraid this nice woman would return her to her tormentor. "It's alright Gabriella I won't give you away. How long have you lived on the street?

"I don't know."

"Never mind. Would you like to work for me? My house is just around the corner. It is a large house and I can use some help. You'll be paid and have a place to eat and sleep."

That's how Gabriella wound up at La Gorda's. She started cleaning the rooms at the bordello. In time La Gorda initiated her in the art of love. When she met Manólo she saw in him a sadness that was not unfamiliar to her. She felt sorrow for his pain and showed him compassion. She became fond of him and gave him her favors gratis.

* * *

MANÓLO LOOKED UP at the broken street lamp. Some ruffians periodically came through the neighborhood and played games tossing small stones at the globes to see who could smash it. He was making a note to have it repaired when the silence was broken by the sound of high heels and quiet laughter. From a distance he recognized Gabriella with a john chuckling and walking toward the alley. He turned away and headed for the shadow but Gabriella spotted him. She let go of her john's arm.

"Manólo come out of the darkness. Come into the light. Let yourself live." She was quite drunk. She put her arms around him and kissed him squarely on the lips, something she never did with a client. "I like you Manólo. You are beautiful and you are honest" she slurred "I respect that. I admire that. I've compromised my life but you've remained true". And she turned back to her john and led him down the alley. Manólo walked on but he felt a twinge of jealousy he could not account for.

*   *   *

LA GORDA'S REAL NAME was Isabella Morros. When she was young and trim she had been the mistress of Baron Alexander Karpov who was the Russian ambassador to Spain. He lavished jewels and furs upon her and set her up in an apartment fully furnished with rich décor. When he was called back to Russia he deeded the apartment to her and she set herself up as a high class escort service catering to the rich and famous. Her girls were more than prostitutes. They were like Geishas given to provide entertainment as well as sex. They often went out with their johns elegantly dressed and were seen with them at public events or at the theater. They were companions and confidants and were rewarded with gifts over and above the price of the ticket.

Isabella had no problem recruiting her girls. They came recommended and she had the choice of the lot. She never took on more than five and they only stayed a year or two, long enough to set aside a little money with which to strike out on their own. At this time there were four ladies at the brothel. La Perla, a tall blond with an engaging smile who had studied at the Beaux Arts in Paris, Birgitta, a Swedish arrival who was shapely and very popular with the clients, Maria, an Italian import with a Mediterranean look, and Gabriella.

Gabriella was the youngest of the four. La Gorda had trained her and gave her the prerogative of turning down a john. So she only went with men she felt comfortable with.

Despite her traumatic initiation, the fact that she enjoyed sex was not a liability and her school girl appearance made her highly desirable. She commanded high fees and only took on high rollers.

La Gorda was now in her forties and had put on a few pounds. She had perfected the art of love making and knew how to turn a trick. She was the Madam and did not have to participate but she found that many men loved her fleshiness and buried their faces in the folds of her body. Business was good at La Gorda's.

*　　*　　*

ON SATURDAY NIGHT the narrow streets were crawling with people. They all seem to be going somewhere. It was like the tide of a flowing river. Strolling groups of young men filled the night with music and laughter. Every now and then an automobile thread its way through the street and everyone scampered for the doorways or flattened themselves up against the walls. After it passed the flow resumed.

From a café somewhere down the street there was the sound of guitars and singing voices and they drew Manólo to them like the warmth of an open fire on a cold night. From the street Manólo could see a crowd of people all standing at the bar or sitting in large groups around tables drinking. Two young men were strumming guitars, standing with one leg on a chair and screeching "Gitana, gitana" and the whole room clapped with delight and sang along. No one paid much attention to the sign over the bar which read "SE PROHIBE CANTAR" singing not allowed.

Off to one side several youths somewhat inebriated and on opposite sides of an intense political argument became loud and agitated. Shouting and name calling followed and one, stumbling all over himself, swung at another who retaliated with a blow which knocked him down with a bloody nose. This precipitated a fight in which they all took part. As happened once in a while things got out of hand and a drunken brawl ensued. Manólo stepped in and struck his chuzo loudly on the floor of the café and it got everyone's attention. He grabbed the two youths who had started it by the collar and took them outside.

"Go home now" he commanded them with authority. "I don't want to see you in here for the next few days. You need to do battle with words, not fists" and shooed them on their way.

*   *   *

LA GORDA STOOD FIRM. The john had pointed to Gabriella. "Her!". Gabriella shook her head from side to side.

"Pick one of the others" La Gorda said. "La Perla really knows how to turn a man on and Birgitta also knows a trick or two".

"I want HER!" he insisted.

"She doesn't want you".

"You let your whores decide?" he snapped back.

"Don't you call my girls whores. This salon is closed to you now. Please leave".

"I'm not leaving. You're in business and I'm a customer." He was obstinate. La Gorda looked over to Maria and gave her a nod. The man might be trouble. Maria went in the kitchen, out the back door and clapped twice.

*   *   *

MANÓLO HEARD THE CLAP and knew where it came from but no one ever clapped in the alley. Something must be wrong he thought and hurried to the brothel.

"You will leave now!" Manólo ordered the man.

The man was incensed. "I will call the authorities."

"I AM the authorities. You had better leave before I arrest you and have the Guardia Civil take you away."

The man was livid. He took his hat and his coat and stormed out cursing loud and long. When he was gone the girls surrounded Manólo and kissed him in turn. He was their hero and not bad looking either. He felt proud and took the accolade with humility.

CHAPTER 11

GISELLA OPENED THE DOOR. "Dr. Arroyo, thank you for coming. Pepíto has a fever. He has been complaining of a sore throat and a headache." She showed Dr. Arroyo into the room where her eight year old son was lying in bed. Carlos, Gisella's husband, stood by the open door. "He cried and coughed all night".

The boy was pale, almost blue. Dr. Arroyo took the stethoscope from his satchel and examined him thoroughly listening to Pepíto's breathing, his heartbeats, and the other sounds made by the boy's body. "I don't know" he said and examined him again. Pepíto's eyes were blurry. He had a high fever and his heart rate was abnormally fast. Dr. Arroyo was perplexed. The symptoms did not match anything he had seen before in his twenty years of practice. He was concerned and tried not to show it. "Some tests may be needed so I think we should get the boy to the hospital". "The hospital?" Gisella started to cry and Carlos put his arms around her. "No cause for alarm" the doctor said "just a precaution."

At the hospital Pepíto was diagnosed with the flu, a disease doctors knew little about. They gave him steam inhalations to relieve the pressure on his chest, cupping and mustard plaster. Nothing seemed to help. Within twenty-four hours his condition deteriorated and he became gravely ill. He went from being delirious and thrashing back and forth to lying stiff staring at the ceiling through white eyes. Gisella was beyond desolate. She sat by her son's bed for three days and nights while the fever raged in Pepíto's body and he went in and out of consciousness. Neither Dr. Arroyo nor the hospital doctors were able to analyze the symptoms and come up with a diagnosis. Much as they wanted to they were unable to reassure the boy's mother. She knelt and prayed by his bedside, went to church and lit candles by the shrine of Mary mother of Jesus and prayed again. Pepíto's condition became critical and his life stood on edge like a coin and could fall either way.

The anxiety was great and was compounded by the fact that Pepíto's younger brother Jaime was beginning to exhibit the same symptoms. Carlos and Gisella's lives were in an uproar. They tried hard to keep each other's spirit up despite their own dire concern.

Carlos came into the hospital room and found Gisella slumped in the chair dozing. He bent down and kissed her gently on the cheek. She woke up startled and quickly looked at her son in the bed. Nothing had changed. "You have to go home Gisella. You can't spend your days and nights here. You have to take a break."

"Break from what Carlos?" she snapped "break from what?" There was bitterness in her voice, almost anger. "I have to be with my son".

"What about your other son Gisella? What about Jaime? He's only six . . . He's lying in bed and keeps calling for you. 'Mama! Mama!' I think you should go."

Gisella relented. She kissed Pepíto and gathered her clothes. "You watch over him Carlos. Call me if there is any change". She stood hesitantly by the door then turned and walked out.

At home she found Señora Catalini, an Italian neighbor who had six children of her own, putting a wet cloth on Jaime's forehead. He was burning up. Gisella lifted him into her arms, sat down in the rocking chair and held him while rocking back and forth and singing "Hijo mio, hijo mio" till they both fell asleep. Cradling her son gave her the first sleep she had in several days.

*   *   *

"SEÑORA, SEÑORA, you have to wake up. You have to go to the hospital. They sent for you." Panic seized Gisella. She handed Jaime to Señora Catalini and rushed out the door. Her thoughts were wrapped in black ribbons as she entered the hospital ward. A child is a terrible thing for a mother to lose and in her mind she had lost him. She waited by the nurse's stand for what seemed like an eternity when Dr. Arroyo came out from the ward. He was smiling broadly and the clouds that loomed over the room faded. "He's going to be alright Gisella. His fever broke. He's going to be alright."

She took a big breath. "Oh! Thank God! Thank God! Can I see him?"

"Of course. You know where he is. Just go in." A lightheaded Gisella found Pepíto sitting up in bed. Some color had come back to his face and when he saw his mother he grinned.

"I've been far away Mama. It was beautiful. There were fields of flowers and . . ."

"Hush now son. I'm glad you're back. You've got to rest now."

Whatever it was that struck Pepíto it went as fast as it came. Gisella was overwhelmed with gratitude. "I don't know how to thank you Dr. Arroyo." She took his hand and kissed it several times. "I had nothing to do with it. We can't figure out what he had" he said "maybe your prayers helped." She looked up at the ceiling and crossed herself. Then she took the boy home. No one ever found out what Pepíto had been afflicted with.

*　　*　　*

"SERENO!" It was a shriek rather than a call. "SERENO!" the woman's voice screamed into the night. Manólo came rushing up to the Contessa's compound. He found her standing in front of her portal in her silk embroidered house robe, disheveled and frightened. "Ayuda me!

Ayuda me! Es mi esposo". She took Manólo through the courtyard and into the house, past the servants who had lit all the chandeliers and stood aghast, not knowing what was happening.

Upstairs, in the master bedroom, lay the Count coughing violently and writhing in pain. His skin was blue and a blood-tinged froth gushed from his nose and mouth. Manólo reeled back at the sight and stumbled over Luisa, their daughter, almost knocking her to the ground. He apologized and couldn't help but notice the tears on her face. She was eighteen and the beauty of her eyes made a fleeting imprint on his mind.

"*Llama al hospital Sereno y da te prisa*". She was frantic. Their phone was out of order and they couldn't make the call. The only other phone in the barrio was at La Gorda's and Manólo knew they'd be up most of the night so he rushed there.

It took nearly an hour before the ambulance made its way to the house. By then half the neighborhood was up, some standing in the street, others at the windows. They brought the Count out on a stretcher but when they reached the hospital there were other emergencies and the Count was not seen right away. Had the doctors known that he was the Count de las Torres they would have given him the priority accorded a man of title. But there was no one to speak for him. Lying in the corridor on the intake gurney he coughed violently. His lungs filled with liquid and he suffocated and died. In the corridor. On the intake gurney.

*   *   *

THE CONTESSA STAYED UP ALL NIGHT wondering what had taken her husband and made him so ill. She sat in the velvet covered armchair and surmised that he had food poisoning. Her thoughts went around in circles till she fell asleep.

When in the morning a courier came and informed her of her husband's demise her mouth fell open in disbelief and she let out a loud "NO!" that could be heard in the street below. She asked the courier what had happened but he could not give her any details. She flopped down in the chair, cupped her head between her hands and sighed deeply, incomprehensibly. Without warning, in one night, her life had changed and she tried to assess the consequences. The Count had been much older than she. She had married the title as much as the man. He had taken his rank in stride but she held it as a mark of nobility and acted accordingly. She enticed the Count to attend more social events than he would have liked, gala dinners and ballroom dances and insisted he wear the several medals he had been given but had never earned. The Contessa had dominated him. Now she felt bereft. But she knew her stalwart personality would handle her distress with a decorum suited to the occasion.

When the word got out that the Count had died the neighbors were distressed. He had been a prominent and respected presence in the Barrio. The portal was draped in black. So was the Contessa who cried crocodile tears and conducted herself as would a grieving widow. But she carried her loss with more dignity than sorrow.

CHAPTER 12

IT WAS 1917. The U.S. had entered the war and the Russian revolution was taking place. Ideological conflict between Spaniards who were for a parliamentary democracy and revolutionary socialists culminated in street demonstrations and fights. Spaniards were always at opposite ends of the political spectrum and they were not loath to confront each other violently on every occasion.

There was not much room left for anything else and no one paid much attention to the account of an unusual sickness reported earlier in the year by a Spanish wire service to Reuters London headquarters:

> *"A strange form of disease of epidemic character has appeared in Madrid."*

*   *   *

ALTHOUGH THEY DIDN'T KNOW IT the virus had already found its way into the Barrio. The rapidity with which the epidemic invaded was overwhelming. People who were fine in the morning turned blue and died by nightfall. Death was everywhere and it spread like black ink from neighborhood to neighborhood. When her coachman fell victim the Contessa was overwrought. It seemed as though it mattered more to her than when her husband died some days ago.

In the next few weeks the scene repeated itself in different habitats, sometimes in the daytime but more often at night and Manólo found himself running from one end of the barrio to the other alongside doctors, Dr. Arroyo among them, and nurses who wore face masks for protection, helping carry stretchers, and consoling the ones who remained behind.

The sirens brought an ambulance that took Marcella and her seventy-two year old mother, as her husband Fidel beat his fists against the stone wall of their compound. Four women making a quilt were struck and three of them died within hours. Manólo was beside himself. There were so many screams of desperation coming from windows and courtyards. He had gotten to know and become fond of the people in his barrio. They were like his flock and so many were carried away on stretchers. Some came back but most didn't. Somehow the flu spared Gabriella and the bordello and Manólo found respite in her bed and the warmth of her body.

*　*　*

THERE WAS AN EPIDEMIC. The daily paper El Diario called it the Spanish flu but it had come from elsewhere. It was raging all over Madrid and had even spread to many parts of Spain. The disease began with a cough, then increasing pain behind the eyes and ears. Body temperature, heart rate, and respiration escalated rapidly. In the worst cases, pneumonia quickly followed and brought them to an end. There was panic all over the city and ambulances screeched through the streets siren blasting away.

The children didn't understand and skipped rope to the rhyme:

I had a little bird,
Its name was Enza.
I opened the window,
And in-flew-enza.

As the days went by it became clear that the flu had spread throughout Europe and was making more victims than the war which was still raging on the western front. In the barrio a great many residents caught the disease and died within days. The drizzle and the rain which had set in during the early days of the epidemic continued fitfully, rendering it difficult to maneuver through the narrow streets.

The flu was highly contagious early in the illness, even before symptoms appeared. The Council of the Elders ordered strict quarantines to prevent its spread and it befell upon Manólo to enforce the quarantine. You didn't have to talk the people into abiding by the quarantine and to remain indoors. They were terror stricken and went out as little as possible. But some youths expressed their fear, anger and frustration by using tick tacks on the windows, tearing down gates and beating the porches with planks. Manólo had to chase them out of his bailiwick.

The poorer sections of the Barrio were the hardest hit. Entire families lay prostrate with fever and despair. Anatolia, an 11 year old, was nursing her sick parents and seven year old brother. When the doctor visited he wanted to take some of the family to the hospital, but Anatolia wept bitterly and begged to leave the family there, saying that she was getting along all right and could care for them.

*   *   *

STILL THE DISEASE CONTINUED UNABATED. Before long it spread to Asturias and Manólo's fears were confirmed when he received a letter that his dad Pépé had fallen victim. He went to church and prayed for him, holding his father's chuzo tightly in his hand.

In the three years since he'd been back Amalia had grown used to having Pépé around. It was nice to have a man in the house and she enjoyed spoiling him as she had her children and everyone she knew. In this crisis she remained in control. She cared for him day and night and watched him slowly succumb to the dreadful disease. She wept and prayed and grieved and buried him in the family plot in the cemetery behind the church. It wasn't long after the funeral that some of the members of the procession were stricken in their turn.

Manólo was desolate. Within less than four years he had lost his wife and unborn child, and now his father. That left Cangas del Narcea as dark and empty as Manólo's nights in the Barrio and he felt the void within himself.

*   *   *

WHEN LUISA, the Contessa's daughter, clapped in front of her portal and Manólo came with the keys, she looked at him and shared his grief.

"Sereno" she asked "Como te llamas?" The question had not been posed often.

"Manólo".

"Yo soy Luisa" and there was a connection that had the making of a relationship. She came and went more often than usual just to have Manólo open the door for her. On occasion she would clap just to see him. She'd look at him and see the sadness in his young face and recognize her own and they'd stand under the street lamp without saying a word till Manólo was called elsewhere.

Manólo had been forlorn since the death of his beloved Marie-Carmen and although he didn't have the same feelings for Luisa, he had a strong affection for her. It was clearly mutual and in the midst of the bedlam all around Manólo, seeking solace, sometimes stood in front of her portal and clapped. Luisa came out and they exchanged a few awkward words. Soon the words turned to touch and they hugged and kissed under the street lamp. It was an affection out of need, a need very different for her than for him.

The Spanish Flu raged on and the papers had double headlines, listing the dead from the flu alongside the dead from the war. In the barrio, as elsewhere, people avoided crowded places and the cafés were often empty. Manólo and Luisa took advantage by meeting at the Café Sonora, an elegant place Luisa was used to frequent with her parents on Sundays afternoons. They found relief from the constant turmoil and sat quietly across the way from each other. In this setting Luisa looked different from the young woman he saw so frequently softly bathed under the street lamp. Here he saw her as she was, a lady, the Contessa's daughter, and he knew this relationship had no basis for being. He felt out of place and had little or no conversation that would reach her. But the feeling was there and it made talk unnecessary.

*   *   *

THE STREETS OF MADRID, generally gay and vivid with movement and color, were deserted and motionless. Here and there an occasional automobile was the only sign of life. Churches, schools, and theaters were closed, along with all other places of public amusement. Red Cross nurses were sent in to help fight the influenza. The hospitals were short of space and Sister Maria-Elena and Sister Carolina, two nuns from the Convent of the Holy

Sepulcher, worked makeshift hospitals under tents set up in city squares. Death was a constant presence in the barrio and the death rate was rising. Obituaries were posted on the front page of the daily paper if one was prominent, or listed on page four if one was not.

On November 11th, 1918 Armistice was announced and World War I came to an end. Though much of the joy was weighed down by the epidemic, people ventured out into the streets for the first time in order to celebrate. There was much dancing and singing. Everybody wore a face mask.

* * *

AS MIGUEL HAD SHARED HIS SECRET LIFE with Manólo so Manólo wanted to share Luisa with him. One Sunday he brought Miguel to the Café to meet Luisa and the moment they looked at each other something clicked. It was instantaneous and Manólo couldn't help but notice.

The three of them met on a few occasions and Manólo felt replaced. He saw them avoiding each other's eyes so as not to offend him but he knew that they were a better match. They spoke at arm's length lest the spark that had been ignited become visible. But Manólo saw and Manólo knew and he was ready to yield to his friend. It took a lot of convincing to overcome Miguel's reticence but he finally did and started to take Luisa out.

They had a lot in common and talked constantly. They talked about the museums they had been to, the theater and the opera, things Manólo had never done. He felt the loss but, despite the affection he had shared with Luisa, he was not in love with her and Miguel definitely was. Manólo couldn't be happier. He shared their happiness and became the third wheel in the triangle. With it their friendship grew. Miguel never revealed to Luisa the clandestine activities he was involved in. Manólo and Miguel now had something more to share, their work and Luisa and it helped Manólo through the fear that permeated the neighborhood, and the nights, always the nights with the incessant claps from all directions which left Manólo in a dither, reeling.

CHAPTER 13

WHEN THE WAR ENDED the flu dissipated and ended as well. Both had left the world shaken and in disarray. The loss of life had been tremendous. It took several years before calm was restored and people began to regain the natural joy of life which was the mettle of the Spanish temperament.

In the two years that followed Miguel and Luisa did not meet in the open. The Contessa did not approve of Miguel. She was a wealthy member of the aristocracy with strong attachments to the Church. He was a member of the intellectual elite, educated and an atheist though his parents were not. He was from the left and she from the right so the lovers kept their relationship in the shadow. They met in less frequented cafés and as much as possible avoided being seen together.

When her husband was alive the Contessa insisted Luisa dress in a manner as to attract potential suitors. Frills and lace and diamond jewelry, all of which Luisa resented. She was not easily manipulated but she loved her father the Count and went along for his sake. She hated being presented as an offering to her mother's highfalutin crowd. Most of the men she met were titled stuffed shirts who bored her to death. Miguel was like a breath of fresh air. He inspired her and made her feel beautiful. In his presence she felt like a bird that had been released from its cage. The Contessa knew Miguel was enamored with Luisa but she pretended not to. She earnestly hoped that her daughter would wake up to her calling and end this undesirable attachment.

Alexander Arroyo was more tolerant than the Contessa and had Miguel bring Luisa home for dinner on occasion. He liked her. She didn't seem spoiled nor constrained by her strict upbringing which was a feat in and of itself. They sat around the table and politics, which was often the subject of dinner conversation, was avoided altogether. She enjoyed the relaxed atmosphere at Miguel's house. There was warmth and laughter which was in great contrast with the decorum her mother required at all times and she was treated like a member of the family.

*   *   *

WHEN THE CONTESSA REALIZED the extent of the involvement she raged and put her foot down. She ordered Luisa not to see Miguel again. But it was an impossible mandate and Luisa disregarded her wishes. The Contessa's discontent grew until one spring day in 1921 she decided to take Luisa out of Miguel's reach. That morning the Contessa de las Torres had the servants pack all their belongings to move to Saragossa where the Contessa's late husband had a mansion. It took place so quickly that Luisa didn't know of her mother's decision till she came home and saw the trunks and suitcases stacked up in the courtyard. She begged, she pleaded, she cried but there was no arguing with the Contessa. She had made up her mind. She wasn't going to let her daughter continue her relationship with a left wing intellectual and mar her standing with the carriage trade. Then there was the fact that the mansion in Saragossa was more elegant and had a more active social set, something she missed in the barrio.

For Luisa the move was heartbreaking. She wasn't even given a chance to see Miguel or say good-by. She was just taken away without warning. A tearful rupture that broke her heart. The move also took place when Miguel Arroyo was away and he only found out about it upon his return. The compound was empty and no one clapped in front of that portal anymore. He needed to understand, to know what had happened and it came in the form of a letter in a pink scented envelope with the trace of a tear next to Luisa's "with all my love" at the end. Miguel wrote back and waited for an answer which never came. He wrote almost every day for the next few months but his letters never reached Luisa. The Contessa intercepted them and Luisa's letters to Miguel wound up in her waste basket. The tether had been cut and would not be reconnected.

Miguel and Manólo shared their distress, Manólo more for Miguel than for himself. On seeing the pain in Miguel's eyes, Manólo reached in his pocket and pulled out an old Egyptian coin which had been given to him as a tip one evening and he thought of it as his talisman. He put it in Miguel's hand and held it in friendship for a long while.

*   *   *

FOR TWO YEARS the compound remained empty. One day Manólo was summoned to the office of the Council of the Elders. As he walked into the age old waiting room he recognized Paola, the old portera at the Contessa's compound. With some apprehension Manólo wondered what they had been called for. Had something been stolen from the premises? There was violent political conflict in Spain between Fascists and Republicans, much bitterness and belligerence resulting in arrests. Often, someone would denounce another just for spite. Had someone pointed a finger at him for some unknown reason Manólo wondered. A totally absurd thought. Nobody even knew he existed.

When they were finally shown into the office of the nominal head of the barrio he sat there behind his desk, a cigar in one hand, and bid them to sit down. He then told them that a person of great importance had purchased the Contessa's residence and would be arriving the next day. That great care had to be taken to give him all the courtesy a nobleman was entitled to. Manólo was puzzled by this admonition. Later, on the way back, Manólo and Paola talked about it but neither could understand the importance of this meeting.

The following day he arrived in his chauffeured limousine, Don Carlos Gomez Di Silva, Grandee of Spain, followed by several cars with his entourage, servants and attendants, and a truck full of suitcases and trunks. When Manólo first saw him he was surprised. Don Carlos did not look like a man of such importance. He was in his late thirties, somewhat effeminate, rather plain, thin and pale, wearing a heavy coat with a fur collar even though the weather was quite pleasant. There was something different in his demeanor and his walk as well.

It is only when he spoke with Miguel that Manólo understood. Don Carlos was of a class which was politically to the right and an avid supporter of the fascists. "Don't be fooled by his appearance" Miguel told him. "He's someone to be reckoned with. His move into the barrio might be a source of trouble".

In the weeks that followed a procession of important men flocked to Don Carlos' residence. Some seemed to be members of an exclusive organization. Others appeared to come to beg favors from one who could grant them.

The Grandee was not the only fascist in the old barrio. In the adjoining barrio the extended family of retired Colonel Marcos Belandro did not hide their leanings. There was an age old building on the Plaza San Ramón, around the corner from the church. On the door there was a brass plaque with strange markings on it and an inverted V with a cross in the middle. The building housed the Club de la Bandera, an exclusive club of like minded men who came twice a month from other sections of Madrid, wearing a tabard embroidered with a crest and a small cross on their lapels. Colonel Belandro joined them as they gathered in the lounge, sitting in armchairs, sifting brandy, discussing politics and relishing the wealth that had endowed them with power. The Grandee never attended. He held court at his residence and the members of the club came to him for an audience.

*　*　*

DAWN WAS JUST BREAKING and daylight filtered through the narrow streets, snaking around corners and stealing the light from the lamp posts. Manólo had spent the last few hours of his shift in a doorway to protect himself from the Levante, a strong wind that came in from the South and blew the litter from last night's paseo all over the place. It had subsided and Tomas, one of the barrio's street cleaners was sweeping it into the gutters where the water from turned on hydrants was washing it into the sewer.

Manólo walked back to his quarters and made himself an omelet with chorizo and champiñones. There was a knock on the door and when Manólo opened it he found Gabriella standing there looking as tired as he felt. She had had a night of it. Manólo greeted her warmly and invited her to share his meal, a meal which could not be called breakfast because it was the last meal of his day not his first.

"Manólo" she said between bites "I came to say good-by".

Manólo was surprised. "You're going some place Gabriella?" he asked.

"No! I'm leaving. I've managed to put a little money aside and I'm thinking of opening a flower shop. I've always loved flowers and making flower arrangements."

"Where will you go?" Manólo inquired.

"I'm going back to Rinconcillo. My stepfather ran off with some younger woman and my mother is alone. I've forgiven her for not standing up for me. I will open my flower shop there. Wish me luck".

Manólo was saddened. "Of course. You deserve a better life. I am glad for you but I will miss you."

They finished eating, washed the dishes and put things away together as a married couple might. Then Manólo opened the bed and they laid down side by side. Their relationship was more of warmth than of sex and they slept. The next day she was gone.

Some months later a postcard came followed by a letter and a picture of Gabriella smiling in front of a brightly colored flower shop. It made Manólo happy and he pinned the picture up on the wall next to his bed.

CHAPTER 14

IN 1923 MIGUEL PRIMO DE RIVERA, the Captain General of Catalonia, staged a coup, dissolving the Cortes and establishing a military directory. Miguel hated to have the same first name as Primo de Rivera. De Rivera had suspended the constitution as well as civil liberties and many Spaniards conspired against him. Miguel Arroyo was among them. He had always been political, siding with the Aliadofilos during the war to end all wars, and now there was this military junta that he opposed.

On an afternoon when Miguel and Manólo were sipping wine at a café there was the siren of a police escort and a limousine carrying Primo de Rivera drove by. As his car slowed down at the curve a man came out of a doorway and hurled a rock at him shouting *"Abajo con Ud déspota!"* "Down with you tyrant!" There was a commotion on the street. The secret service rushed the man, knocked him down and beat him with their clubs. A crowd formed with many shouting at the Guardia *"Déja le! Déja le!"* "Let him go! Let him go!" but they continued to hit him till blood ran on the pavement. Miguel stood up and cringed.

"Do you know him?" Manólo asked

"Yes" Miguel answered "his name is Domingo Torrent. He is a communist day laborer who's been in prison several times for sedition". Miguel shrugged and sat down dejectedly. Manólo had not developed a political consciousness yet but in friendship he participated in Miguel's activities.

The hideout had been moved. In a windowless storage space in the back of his compound Miguel had set up a print shop and the room was filled with pamphlets and other subversive material. He had remained in close contact with his friends Cortez and Adolfo. Cortez now turned his poetry into inciting rhetoric and Adolfo oiled the machine and kept everything running smoothly. Manólo joined them. Simón, who was more interested in girls than politics, had moved on. Manólo spend much of his spare time turning the mimeograph machine, making multiple copies of an underground tract they decided to call "*La Verdad*", the truth. Miguel hoped to use the word as a weapon to crush the Falange and was grateful as much for Manólo's help as for the sharing of something which was important to him.

* * *

THE NIGHT WAS UNCOMFORTABLY HOT. The air was thick and humid which made the darkness more dense. Manólo fingered the keys around his neck while walking along the Calle d'Oro. It had become a habit. The keys were like friends. He knew each one of them and as he singled one out, his mind would wander into that residence and the people it housed. He would imagine their lives and weave a whole family history in his imagination. There was so much time during any one night for the silence to be either heavy and burdensome or light and inspiring. These little games Manólo played with himself helped him pass the time.

The silence was suddenly broken by the sound of running steps in the adjoining street. Manólo made a run for it and came upon two young ruffians who had broken into the General Store. There was glass all over the ground.

"*Oigan, párense*" "Hey you" he shouted his night stick raised. They stopped and backed off for a moment. Then out of a doorway came two more hoodlums who pounced on Manólo from behind, struck him on the head and knocked him to the ground. They ripped the purse that was tied to his belt and contained the night's coins and ran off into the darkness.

He hadn't seen it coming and the blow was heavy. His eyes blurred and he almost lost consciousness. He landed with his hand on a piece of glass and had a time getting up. Then he took out his whistle and blew it loud and long. Within minutes neighboring Serenos came from several directions. Manólo gave them an account of the break in and they fanned out back to their quarters on the look out for anyone running through their barrio. Matéo Guzman stayed. He was the

Sereno to the north, a rolly polly middle-aged man who waddled rather than walked and always wore a smile. He had become a friend. Manólo didn't know most of the other Serenos though they came from the same town but they had left Cangas years ago, when Manólo was just a boy. It was obvious that Manólo was shaken. He had a big lump on his head and his hand was bloody. Matéo said he would cover Manólo's beat and walked him to La Gorda's.

When Manólo entered the brothel the ladies of the night vied for the privilege of attending him. Lola and Patricia put an ice-pack on his head while Camilla bandaged his hand and poured him a glass of champagne. He had never met these girls before. They were recent arrivals. Every few years the cast would change. Some would come and others would go.

Manólo felt quite at home at La Gorda's. He often spent the day there in the warm and comforting company of the ladies. They jostled him and teased him but they treated him like royalty. He missed Gabriella with whom he had a special relationship. Even though it was daytime it always looked like the middle of the night. The crystal chandelier in the drawing room, the false antique paintings of reclining nudes over the soft velvet couches with the cushiony pillows. The heavy red and gold drapery hung over the windows to keep out the light of day. It was all meant to seduce.

Manólo wasn't used to drinking champagne. The two glasses went to his head and he stretched out on one of the couches and closed his eyes. Lola and Patricia covered him with a blanket and he fell asleep.

CHAPTER 15

THERE WAS REJOICING in Cangas del Narcea and in the neighboring towns. The harvest had been good and everyone went to church to thank God for the bounty. Then the town square was decorated for a harvest ball and the festivities began. The women in colorful red wool skirts with velvet stripes and elaborate beadwork, the men in traditional garb with corduroy knee pants, all danced to the flute, the bagpipes and the fiddle, jumping with raised arms and twirling till they were dizzy.

Estèfan and Paco drank a gallon of sangria, danced arm under arm, and wound up falling all over each other. Consuela, Estèfan's wife, sat under a tree breast feeding the new baby. She had put on weight with the birth of her fourth child. Fuencísla, Paco's wife, was barren and childless and she tried to make up for it by helping Consuela with her children.

They were startled when some teenagers exploded firecrackers nearby and the baby began to cry. Consuela handed the baby to Fuencísla and she rocked him back and forth while the fireworks lit up the sky in brilliant colors of yellow, red and gold. When it got late, the women took the children home and the men continued dancing alone or with each other drinking from botas, leather wine bags. Many wound up sleeping it off on the grassy knoll while others had to be helped home singing loudly and off key.

The next day the women set up tables all around the square and mounds of food were laid out, roast suckling pig, fabadas and bean stew with casks of cider to wash it all down. Families gathered together in feasting and merriment and many men made love to their wives that night. The revelry lasted for two full days.

*   *   *

CONSUELA PUT HER WET WASH INTO A BUCKET and carried it out to the back of the house. Her small children, raggedly dressed but chubby and smiling, played around her skirts while the baby slept in the nearby crib. She was hanging the sheets on the clothes line when the shrill sound of the mine's siren pierced the air. It sent a chill down her spine and she dropped everything. She picked up the baby and, with the other children in tow, she joined the women who were running along the path toward the mine. It was not the first time but no one gets used to accidents and no one is immune from fear.

When they reached the mine the siren was still blasting. There had been an explosion and a fire had broken out. Flames came roaring up the shaft of hole number six which was covered with a seething mass of burning timbers. Thirty six men were trapped and the terrible shrieks of women screaming echoed all around. Consuela found Fuencísla in the crowd and they held the children tight and tried to calm their fear while being unable to calm their own.

A bucket brigade was organized to extinguish the fire and it took several hours to bring it under control. A number of men who were at the mouth of the tunnel bellowed down the shaft and some thought they heard sounds. Cheers went up from the assembled crowd of women and children. A sentiment of relief was experienced for the first time since morning and there was hope that the men would be found alive. Efforts were again made to call to those below, but there was so much confusion around the mouth of the shaft, so many people gathered there, and all so anxious to see what was going on, that it was impossible.

Another loud call was made. Breathless silence was observed but no answering voice was heard and hope died away. Amador Stanzio, an old time miner who had seen his share of mining accidents, volunteered to go down the hole. A derrick was set over the shaft and a bucket was securely fastened to the rope. He hooked on his lamp and commenced the perilous descent. Fifteen minutes after he disappeared he again reached the surface gasping for air. Halfway down the pit he found obstructions which prevented his further descent but the brattice had not burned and the air was perfectly good. Several men would have to go down to remove the obstructions. There was always the danger that the digging might burst the air pocket that was created to hold the water back and supply the miners with oxygen. It took hours and the sweat of many to cut through until the mine ceiling was breached.

As time ticked away and the men were digging at the cave-in fears grew stronger and with each passing hour the chances of survival became less and less. Then it started to rain making the digging more difficult. Still the women waited in desperation wondering how many of them would become widows that day. Rescue shafts were measured to be 180 feet down and the rain hampered the rescue efforts. Consuela and Fuencísla huddled together and prayed that it would not take their husbands. They made silent vows to Christ to undertake some charitable work if they were spared. Miners from other shafts prayed silently for their comrades in the mine.

Some of the Quonset huts around the mine were set up with cots, others with tables and benches. Among the confusion Manólo's mother Amalia and his aunt Rosa found Consuela and her children. As did many others they had brought food for the work parties. A makeshift kitchen was arranged and Amalia took charge of feeding the multitude of workers, wives and children, out of cauldrons of hot black-bean soup. For forty-eight hours teams of rescuers took turns in the hole in the desperate hope of there still being some life in the bowels of hell. Women stood vigil day and night as hope fizzled. Convinced that the men in the mine would not be recovered alive the horrible truth began to sink in that they were in fact bereaved.

On the third day, when all hope had almost vanished, sixteen year old Enrique Pasqual and Amador Stanzio heard sounds deep in the mine as of heavy pounding some distance from the bottom of the shaft. The only hope for the trapped men is their having shut themselves out entirely from the draft. Seventy or eighty yards into a gangway Enrique and Amador came to a jammed door and heard moans and groans on the other side. With their hatchets they hacked away till it tumbled. They shuddered at what they saw. Twenty four men were buried under the debris of falling rock and timbers. The twelve black faced survivors were stunned overcome by the gases.

When word reached the surface there was a commotion and an outcry from the women who rose to their feet and ran toward the mine exit hoping that their man was among the survivors. One after the other the miners were brought out of hole number six, all looking like ghosts with their coal-blackened faces. The exhausted men who had survived and endured were carried out bodily. Consuela let out a scream when they brought Estèfan out on a stretcher. She ran to him tears streaming down her face "Estèfan, Estèfan . . . Oh! my God. He's alive." He had succumbed to smoke inhalation but he would be alright. Three more half-conscious men were brought out on stretchers. Fuencísla had given up hope when they brought Paco out. He had been wedged in between two fallen beams. His left leg had been crushed and he was somewhat in a daze. He looked up, smiled at her and reached for her hand. When the last survivor was brought out wails tore through the air, the keening of women whose hopes were shattered. One by one the bodies of the dead miners were brought out of the tunnel on biers which were deposited on the ground each eliciting the scream of a woman who recognized a husband or a father. The tragedy was enormous and the night that followed was black as coal and filled with the tears of widows and orphans.

*   *   *

WITH THE PAIN OF THEIR DEAD COMRADES in their hearts the anger of the miners reigned supreme. The conditions in the mine were dangerous and the management had knowledge of this yet did nothing. This was not the first accident if it could be called that. The mining company, whose headquarters were in Oviedo, had not taken the normal precautions for the safety of the miners. The company was owned by wealthy individuals who were never there but had foremen whose jobs depended on maximizing output at minimum cost and keeping the miners in line. Enraged miners with their wives marched on the mining office shouting and shaking their fist. The foreman, a giant of a man with arms like rubber tires, tried to calm them down but at the core, he agreed with them. They came together and marched into the office, past the stunned secretary, some fifty or so black faced miners, to confront the manager. Threats were made and words were exchanged. It almost came to blows.

The pale-faced manager cowered behind his desk and promised to take their grievances back to the company.

Fuencísla did not go with the men to the mining office. She stayed with Paco as Doctor Banderos put Paco's leg in a cast. It was a bad multiple fracture and the doctor told him it would be several weeks before he could walk again. He also told him that he would probably wind up with a limp which would prevent him from going back down in the mines. Paco was distressed. How would he be able to support his wife? The company only paid minimal compensation for the death or injury of its workers. Fuencísla tried to relieve his anxiety with "we'll manage. I can always take in laundry, ironing and sewing". He didn't have any children and, at this point, he was glad he didn't.

*　　*　　*

THE CEMETERY WAS OVERFLOWING with families who had lost a dear one to the tragedy. Twenty-four graves were lined up side by side, with black veiled relatives all around. There were men, women and children, young and old, stretching to hear the few words Father Domingo Casperon was offering to console the grieving crowd:

"To all of you who are in mourning I mourn with you. To die suffocating in the bowels of the earth plunging beloved wives into widowhood and children into parental bereavement is more suffering and pain than anyone should have to endure. Yet it is said 'Our Father who art in Heaven hallowed be thy name thy kingdom come thy will be done . . ." The assembled congregation took up the prayer "on earth as it is in heaven . . . for thine is the kingdom, and the power, and the glory, for ever and ever." Father Casperon concluded with "I hope and pray that the Lord will sedate and comfort the bereaved relatives of the deceased and prove himself to be the Provider for the widow and the Father of the fatherless. Amen."

In the next few days El Minero Vizcaino, the miners' newspaper, reported on the accident in great detail accusing the mine owners of criminal neglect and demanding reparations for the victims. The central feature was a scathing article by Dolores Ibárruri who wrote under the name of La Pasionaria. She was the daughter of an Asturian miner and from childhood had been used to abject poverty and violent political strikes. In her columns she battled to gain amelioration of the living and working conditions of her people. She would later become the voice of struggling workers throughout Spain and a major player in left wing politics.

*   *   *

WHEN THE FIRST LIGHT OF DAWN came up Manólo made his way back to his quarters with a weariness that he was now familiar with. He was no longer the fresh young man from the country. His ten years of walking the night gave him a strong pair of legs but it took its toll on his shoulders and he had a tendency of slouching. Though still quite young he had taken to shave only every three days and almost always sported a stubble which gave him a virile look. The Ladies of the Night found it very attractive.

When he came into the courtyard and picked up the morning paper in front of his door the words MINING DISASTER IN ASTURIAS struck him in the face. He leaned against the wall and read what was the headline in every paper throughout Spain. Some twenty-four miners had lost their lives and twelve had survived with injuries ranging from minor to life-threatening. Manólo was distressed and slumped down to the ground in front of his door. His thoughts rushed to Paco and Estèfan and the many men he had befriended when he worked with them in the pit. He grabbed his coat and quickstepped to La Puerta del Sol on the Plaza San Ramón where Serenos often met to play dominos or talk about the events of the day. Sometimes a new boy in town would be the center of attraction as Manólo had been many years ago.

As he entered the Plaza Manólo could see the intense activities at the Café. More than a dozen men of all ages, all wearing the Sereno's loose mantle, sitting or standing around, talking excitedly with great concern, each carrying a copy of La Prensa, or Ahora, or La Nación. They were all from Cangas. They all had family, brothers, uncles and nephewswho still worked in the mines. Manólo crossed and entered the Café shaking hands here and there with his colleagues who fretted over the fate of their loved ones. Luis and Emilio agreed to go to the Servicio de

Correos y Telegrafos and wire for news of the victims of the disaster.

In the next few days you could see grim Serenos in many barrios wearing a black armband and a somber face.

CHAPTER 16

THE YEARS WENT BY and the causes changed. In 1930 an alliance of convenience between political factions brought huge crowds into the streets of Madrid and ended the dictatorship. A Republic was proclaimed and everyone breathed a sigh of relief. But the period of tranquillity that followed didn't last. The country was divided, politically, socially and economically. Though a republic in name, the new government was in the hands of right wing conservatives and well down the road to fascism. Many Spaniards were convinced that the only way to stop this from happening was by making a revolution.

The University was a hotbed of dissidence. Miguel had obtained a degree in political science and had become assistant professor at the University. He was very popular and as he walked through the quad the students greeted him with respect and often a great deal of affection. Many female students had a crush on him. He had an engaging personality and could be found almost any afternoon at a table in the University cafeteria, surrounded by enthusiastic students. His lectures gave him a podium for sharing his convictions. There was much heated discussion in his class and it echoed through the halls. The administration was wary of professor Miguel Arroyo and often monitored his class. When they did he tempered his tone and softened his rhetoric and they couldn't pin him down. Though not in league with the administration, most of the rest of the faculty kept a low profile for fear of losing their job.

* * *

WHEN IN 1932 MIGUEL'S FATHER RETIRED and his parents moved back to Sevilla where they originally came from, Miguel wound up alone which turned out to be convenient. *"La Verdad"* had taken on importance. It had become an underground paper and needed more space so the print shop was moved from the storage room to a two room shack in back of the compound. Each printing was in the thousands, in addition to the tracts and broadsides which were handed out and posted on street walls. Cortez was no longer with Miguel. He had married and moved to Pamplona. Adolfo, who had graduated from the University with a degree in electrical engineering, was still there and there were two new recruits, Pastor and Bernardo. Miguel had caught them one night writing anti-government graffiti on some walls, offered them a better way to express their anger, and enlisted them in the cause.

Though not with any degree of regularity, *"La Verdad"* appeared on café tables, on park benches, and under doorways a little all over Madrid at least once a week. It expressed the frustration of people throughout Spain who were furious at the fascism the regime was headed for. The message was clear and it touched off thousands of workers on a buyer's strike. The impetuous Spaniards manifested their discontent. They stayed away from buses, shops, bars and cafés, even newspapers. Students demonstrated on campus and on the streets. The Police patrolled the city in trucks, cars and on horseback. The outbreak of violence was always just a thread way, in Madrid as in many other parts of the country.

In Asturias the harsh reality of the mining community had produced a tradition of cooperation and unity. Asturians are a hardy lot. Whenever there was trouble, Asturian miners were warriors on the front-line of the struggle. In March 1934 they joined a Workers' Alliance in the mining town of Mieres, 20 km south-east of Oviedo.

*   *   *

THE NIGHT WAS RATHER QUIET. Manólo stopped under a street lamp, reached into his vest pocket and took out his watch. It was a few minutes past 4 A.M. He held his chuzo up to the light and looked at the bull's head carved on the knob. For a brief instant he saw himself standing in front of his father Pépé and recalled the glimmer in his eyes as he handed Manólo his staff. This thought made him sad and somewhat unnerved. He wished he had taken up smoking. Most of the Serenos he knew smoked and it helped them relax on dark and lonesome nights.

Some whispers brought him back to the lamp post. He stepped into the shadow and stretched his keen ears to the oncoming footsteps. From a distance Manólo saw two young thugs tearing down La Verdad posters and tracts from the walls. With a swift rap on the pavement he surprised them. "What do you think you're doing?"

The shorter one seemed brash. His hair was slicked down and he looked like he hadn't been shaving very long. He couldn't be more than seventeen Manólo thought yet he defiantly answered "Nothing!"

"What do you mean nothing"? Manólo said, irritated by the young man's audacity. "I'm the Sereno here and you're not from this barrio."

The boy straightened up trying to make himself taller than he was. "My name is Arturo Belandro and I am the son of Colonel Marcos Belandro" he spat out with aplomb.

"I don't care who you are. I am the authority here and you are destroying public property. Now get on home both of you and don't let me catch you doing mischief in my barrio again or I'll hold you for the Guardia Civil. They'll know how to deal with young punks like you." Manólo raised his chuzo menacingly and the two of them took off in the dark.

*   *   *

ARTURO BELANDRO was the only son of Colonel
Marcos Belandro. Cuddled and spoiled by his mother
Victoria and disciplined to the limit by his father he was
a brazen young man and at his young age he had already
been marked by street brawls and arrests, each time
rescued by his influential father. The confrontation was
the same on each occasion. The Colonel would call his
son into his study and lecture him sternly admonishing
him for his behavior.

"What have you done again? I cannot keep covering
for you. I was called by an orderly of the Guardia Civil
about your street activities." The Colonel's voice was
harsh but you could tell that underneath it he was proud
of his only son, his heir who would continue the line.
"You're putting a strain on our family name. I know you
consider yourself a man. But you're still a boy and you're
a Belandro. We do things differently. We take power from
the top, not in the streets. Now stay out of trouble". Arturo
pretended to be sorry and the Colonel dismissed him as
on past occasions.

*　　*　　*

MANÓLO CAME HOME as the first of light of dawn
appeared in the sky. He poured himself a drink, took
a shower and changed. The early morning sun was
pleasant. He brought a chair out into the courtyard
and sat down with a book. In the years they had been
friends Miguel Arroyo had guided Manólo's education

126

by providing him with reading material. Manólo had started with romance novels and moved on to the classics. He had not become an erudite but he had become a reader. He spent the early part of most mornings reading and sipping a sangria. Now, because of his involvement with Miguel's activities, he had begun to read non-fiction books. and followed political events in weekly periodicals.

At 10 AM he walked to the Café Gijón with his morning paper and had a Cortado and a croissant. Was it a dream or was it a small article about Cangas del Narcea in the morning paper that made him nostalgic and think of going back to Asturias for a spell to revisit the playground of his childhood? He thought of the days in the Sidrería when he was a young miner, of the feeling of kinship, clinking glasses and singing Asturian drinking songs with the men. He thought of the gossiping about girls with his friends and the pranks they played on each other. Most of the time it was Paco, the joker. Like the time he fell off his bike and blackened two of his front teeth to pretend they had been knocked out by the fall. Or when he went into great detail about the exploits he had with this or that girl, exploits which had never happened. Carefree days that seemed so far away now. What started out as a fleeting thought took on greater dimensions. His mind wandered through the fields of corn, the tall grasses and above all the sky, the vast expanse of the Asturian sky. Something he missed most of all. Though he had not held his mother Amalia in his arms in a long time he had held her in his heart and longed for her warmth and the love of which she gave so freely. As he drank his morning coffee the images of the long family table and the people gathered around it flitted by in his memory and the longing grew. He knew he had to go

Matéo Guzman never married and had no children. So when he retired his nephew Marcus took over his barrio. Manólo had gotten Marcus to cover for him on occasion and he arranged for him to do so again so he could go back to Asturias.

*   *   *

HE FOUND HIMSELF ON THE TRAIN heading north. He sat by the window and thought. This was only the third time he rode the train. He remembered that first time when he came to Madrid to be a Sereno. The train ride was a joy and the view of the landscape whizzing by out the window had given him a glow. He was young then and saw it as discovering the world, expanding his horizons. Everything was new and he was full of the anticipation of an adventure, a new life, a new beginning. He had from childhood projected such heroic cartoon images of his future as a Sereno that he was quickly deflated by the reality.

The second was when he returned from Cangas, delirious with happiness, having married his love Marie-Carmen. The images of this second train ride were not out the window. They were in his heart. Everything outside of him was a blur. There was love and sadness and hope, and a prayer to Jesus that it would all work out. Why didn't it? "Why did God let me lose the boy I will never get to see?" It was a question he wouldn't allow himself to answer lest he give up Jesus and God altogether. And he wasn't prepared to do that.

He was much older now and, having spent so much of his waking hours in the darkness of the Madrid night, he looked at the scenery with different eyes. The landscape was vivid and beautifully alive. The fields of corn and wheat and barley spread out in all directions bathed by the warm summer sun. Windmills speckled the horizon. Manólo felt a sense of release, of being able to breathe with the fullness of his being. Unlike Madrid where the nights were often heavy and weighed him down, he felt light and easy.

In the years that passed the trains had become much faster and within several hours he was looking out at the Cantabrian Ranges going over the Cordillera mountains through the *Puerto de Leitariego*. Once through the pass the train whizzed by Villablino, an abandoned railway station which shuttled the miners to and from Ponferrada many years ago. Once in a while billows of smoke from the locomotive obstructed his view and took him down into the shaft of the mine where he had spent a portion of his youth. Passing Mestas, the nearest town to Cangas del Narcea, things began to look familiar and Manólo wondered what he would find, what changes had occurred after so many years.

*　　*　　*

HE HAD WRITTEN TO PACO and asked him to alert his mother of his coming. When the train pulled in Paco was waiting on the platform and came to him with hands extended. They embraced, kissed on both cheeks then stepped back to look at each other. Paco was no longer the brash young man who laughed and joked and made pranks. He was paunchier and somewhat debilitated by the mining accident that had left him with a limp.

"It's good to see you my friend". There was real warmth and sincerity in that hackneyed greeting. "It's been so many years". They stood in silence for a moment, as if there was so much to say that they didn't know where to begin. They walked arm in arm to a Model T Ford parked in back of the station. Manólo stared in disbelief. "It's mine." Paco affirmed. "They call it a Tin Lizzie. I got it with the money I received from the mining accident. There was such an uproar after that disaster that the mining company paid compensation to the widows and the men who were injured. I need a car because of my limp. It helps me get around."

On the way back to town they relaxed a bit and recovered some of their past comradeship. They talked about "the good old days" and how their lives had changed over the years. Manólo detected some bitterness in Paco at not having children. It made for an empty nest. "So what are you doing these days?" Manólo asked.

"I am an organizer for the local miner's union. What with my bum leg I couldn t go back to the mines or follow in your footsteps and be a Sereno so . . .".

"That's better than choking on the coal dust in the mine" Manólo remarked. "And it's an important job". Manólo was impressed.

"Important yes. But dangerous as well. You should know what's going on. The company hired a number of thugs to come down on union organizers with their billy clubs. Last week they cornered Guido and Martel who are leaders of the North Slope miners and had attended a union organizing meeting. They beat them bloody with their truncheons. The miners won't take this anymore. The union is strong and this kind of tactic just makes more miners join. There's a lot of anger out there and something is going to happen. It's just a matter of where and when". Paco talked on and on as if he had a need to pour out the weight on his mind. Manólo listened for all the times he wasn't there for his friend.

* * *

AMALIA COULD NOT COME to the station but she stood on the porch by the open door with arms outstretched and tears running down her face. It was a welcoming he had longed for. They sat on the old rocking chairs looking out on the fields and talked. Manólo wanted to know about things that happened since he went away. She hesitated but he insisted. He wanted to know everything in great detail. So Amalia told him how she sat by the bed and held Marie-Carmen's hand at the last. She didn't mention how long and painful her labor had been. "I lied to her" Amalia said. "The baby was still-born but I told her she had a fine healthy boy. She smiled and said 'Manólo will be very happy'". It was the last thing she said.

Manólo wiped his eyes. "I didn't want to talk about these things Manólo. It brings back sad times and it was long ago". She put her arms around him. I'd rather talk about the days when you stood in front of the whole clan and read your father Pépé's letters from Madrid". In the next hour or so they ran through the years before and after Manólo left home. Then they sat in silence for a long while until the noon church bells brought them back to the present. Manólo needed to shake the sadness from his body so he leaned over and kissed his mother then got up and went to town.

Cangas del Narcea had not changed in all the time he was away. It was as if time had stood still. The cafés on the square still had a few old-timers sipping sidra and playing checkers. All in the slow paced leisure of the warm summer day. The play was the same only the actors had changed. A new generation of teenagers laughed and played and dreamt about being a Sereno without knowing what it meant. Manólo felt ambivalent. Should he tell these youths about the reality of the Sereno, about the nights, the solitude, the loneliness? About the thousands of miles walking from one end of the barrio to the other, back and forth, back and forth, like a lion in a cage or an inmate in solitary confinement pacing his cell with only a small ray of light coming from a transom? No! He thought. Let them live out their fantasy. The reality will come soon enough and when the time comes they will have no choice. They would have to go.

*   *   *

THE SCENE WAS FAMILIAR to Manólo. It was like a painting on the wall of his past. Eight people sitting on benches on both sides of the table, all men, Paco and Estèfan among them, Mama Garcia at the head dishing out the stew in plates that passed around. Between the rattling of the dishes and the silverware the conversation was focused on the problems in the mines and the lack of concern by the absentee owners. Paco, who was a veteran in the war against the bosses and had a bum leg to prove it, had been chosen to represent the Cangas miners at the Workers' Alliance in Mieres. Manólo stood out as a Sereno in their midst but in many ways the nights in the barrio were almost as dark as the bottom of the pit. Still he felt a nip of jealousy at the camaraderie and solidarity of the miners. They were like a family. It made him aware that he didn't belong. He was a different man, a solitary man, an outsider. The past had outdistanced him.

After the meal the men dispersed and Paco, Estèfan and Manólo headed for the Sidrería. On the way, there were young miners walking arm over shoulder or arm in arm. It brought back memories, so many years ago, the picnics, the dances, the fellowship. They sat down, drank and talked over old times and the friendship that had bound them together through the years despite the distance between them. "I'm driving to Mieres tomorrow for a meeting of the delegates of the Workers' Alliance" Paco said. "I'd love for you to come along. I can use the company". They raised their glasses and clinked them to being together again.

When the church bell rang the call for the Vespers service Manólo felt the need to join the women in the holy enclave. He genuflected, crossed himself, and knelt in one of the pews. Words and chants resonated throughout this mediaeval edifice but they came to Manólo as a jumble of sound. He got up and sneaked out the back door. The crosses of the cemetery struck him in the face. He knew the cemetery was behind the church and the grave of his Marie-Carmen was there but he had shut it out of his mind. He hesitated then began to look until he found it.

MARIE-CARMEN GARCÍA GARCÍA
1898-1915
daughter of Olivia, wife of Manólo
"She died too soon!"

Marie-Carmen's face came before him, as vivid as if she were there and he felt a surge of love. Then it came to him. This was also the grave of the baby that didn't live long enough to be named. And he fell to his knees and wept. There was sadness but there was also a sense of release, of forgiveness, making peace with the past. Manólo went back into the church and lit a candle in reverence to the memory while holding Marie-Carmen's locket close to his chest, a locket that he had always worn around his neck.

*   *   *

MIERES WAS A BUSTLING TOWN. There were people on the streets, shops and buildings with offices in them. The Workers' Alliance was on the third floor of one of those buildings. Paco and Manólo walked up the stairs Paco dragging his leg a bit. Carla, the lady at the desk greeted Paco warmly. He had obviously been there many times.

"They've started the meeting. Go on in".

As he walked in several men slapped Paco on the back and welcomed him. He introduced his long time friend as an observer. It was in many ways the same scene as at Mama Garcia's, a long table but this was a conference table of polished mahogany and the men sat on comfortable leather chairs. There was only one woman there, Dolores Ibárruri, the columnist for El Minero Vizcaino. She was not there as an observer or as a reporter. She was there as a strong advocate for the miners' cause. Each man was a delegate from one of the mines of Asturias and each had a list of grievances he wanted addressed. All agreed that they had to take a united stand and not flinch from their demands. "We organize and strike. If needed we fight". The meeting lasted an hour and ended with everyone agreeing and shaking hands. Then they all gathered at the local restaurant for lunch.

On the way out Paco introduced Manólo to Dolores Ibárruri. She was in her mid-thirties, had a chock-full of black hair tied in a bun, and was fairly attractive. But there was a masculine side of her which was dominant. Manólo was impressed by her compelling personality and her devotion to the cause. They spoke briefly and when Manólo told her he was a Sereno in Madrid she posed most of the questions the teenagers of Cangas asked their parents, and listened attentively to his answers. Then she looked at her watch and indicated she had to get back to the paper.

The next few days were spent with Amalia, with Estèfan and his family and with many of the people that he had known. When it came time to take the train back to Madrid Manólo was heavyhearted. He wanted to stay under the bright blue sky of Asturias where the air was free and the fragrance of flowers was everywhere. But something was pulling him back to his barrio. Though they didn't know it, though they didn't know him, the denizens were his family as much as those in Cangas and they needed him to blanket the night with the security of his presence while they slept. It was a tug but he had engaged himself long ago and there was no turning back.

CHAPTER 17

IT WAS SUNDAY, the day of the Feast of the Sacred Heart, and it had become more than a religious holiday. It had become the expression of the Church's support for a fascist regime. In many areas of the city white banners stamped with the sacred heart hung from windows and balconies.

The Falange's Blue Shirts, an organized fascist group modeled after Mussolini's Black Shirts and Hitler's Brown Shirts ran through the streets shouting *revolución, revolución'* and painting swastikas on walls. Arturo had been inducted into the group and become one of the leaders. This pleased his father as the Blue Shirts were a para-military unit and anything that had to do with the military got his approval. But the Blue Shirts were known to use violence in an effort to overthrow the existing administration and take power.

Supporters of the government did not remain idle. They took to the streets and confronted the Blue Shirts. Gangs of breathless young men in rope-soled shoes tore through the neighborhoods cutting up the banners wherever they saw them. Every now and then the two sides met coming from different directions and the fight was on. Rocks thrown, clubs wielded, and blood on the cobblestones until the Guardia Civil and the Army came and took control. But there was bitter hostility and the conflict of opposing ideas was everywhere. Five churches were burned.

As a shouting crowd swept along the Gran Via, a man suddenly arose from a café table crying *"Viva Cristo Rey!"* "Long Live Christ the King!" The crowd made for him but he fought them off with powerful squirts from a pale blue soda siphon. They wrecked the restaurant instead. Angry youths broke windows and went on a rampage, ransacking empty fascists residences. Manólo's barrio was not spared. When Manólo came on duty and saw the vandalism and damage that had taken place he felt sorry. His sentiments were with the ones causing the havoc but this was his flock and he felt protective of them all regardless.

In all the fracas there were still papers that came out and provided news of violent disturbances from other parts of Spain. Despite this political upheaval fearless Madrilleños still met in cafés and the average Spaniard still took his daily siesta.

* * *

IT WAS EARLY TUESDAY MORNING. Manólo had just come off his night shift. It had been a cold night and he was warming his hands on a cup of coffee when a messenger came with a portentous official envelope. In it was a formal notice for him to appear at one o'clock that afternoon at the Officina Central de la Guardia Civil near the courthouse in downtown Madrid. Concerned and apprehensive he donned his Sunday clothes and headed downtown. When he arrived a dozen Serenos were already there and others were arriving separately or in pairs. He knew most but not all of them. They were milling around, whispering and speculating on why they had been called. After a long wait they were ushered into what looked like a classroom with seats in rows and a desk up front. The waiting was suspenseful. Then a stern looking middle-aged man with close-cropped hair and a manicured black mustache entered from a side door. He wore the spiffy green uniform of the Guardia Civil with a golden eagle on each shoulder. The room came to a hush as the officer stood straight-faced behind the desk looking at the assembled men without saying a word. The silence was heavy.

"My name is Fernando Salazar. I am the Capitàn de la Guardia" he addressed them as a group "and YOU are officers of the law". He then reached in a folder he had placed on the desk and pulled out a few broadsides. "Do you know who is putting out these treasonous sheets?" He stood motionless and his eyes shifted from man to man. "DO YOU KNOW WHO IS PUTTING OUT THESE TREASONOUS SHEETS?" he repeated loudly furrowing his brow. "They call it *'La Verdad'* and it is intended to arouse the people against the government". He stiffened and glanced around the room. Holding up several tracts he continued "This must be STOPPED. We have word that it comes from one of your barrios. You know your barrios. You know everything that goes on in them."

Manólo trembled and shifted his weight nervously. Although he sat in the fourth row he thought that the Capitàn had looked pointedly in his direction. He felt the words were leveled at him. He had never really given it a thought. He was an accomplice. He could be arrested for it. He could be imprisoned or worse. It had never entered his mind. He was just helping out a friend, a friend who could be shot for treason. He shuddered.

"Remember, you are an OFFICER OF THE LAW" the Capitàn repeated for emphasis "and you have to report anything suspicious". Manólo had also never thought of himself as an officer of the law. He thought of himself as the guardian and protector of the residents in his barrio. "Anyone who fails to do so will be severely punished" the Capitàn continued. "I expect you to do your duty. Look carefully among your flock for anyone whom you suspect might be printing and distributing this seditious material and turn the information in to us. That's all" and he left abruptly the way he came.

When the meeting broke up the Serenos walked out shrugging their shoulder not knowing why they had been targeted. They broke into small groups and headed for nearby cafés to drink and discuss the false accusation. Only Manólo knew it wasn't and he ducked out and went home quietly.

CHAPTER 18

POLICE OFFICERS ON FOOT and on horseback stood on all corners of the large main plaza in Mieres. The square was filled with miners, field and factory workers who had come from the entire region to hear her. The authorities anticipated trouble and posted guards all around. There was a podium and a loud cheer erupted from the crowd as Dolores Ibárruri, La Pasionaria mounted the platform. Her devotion to the Spanish working class was absolute and she had become a known figure in radical political circles. Tall, handsome, and with a great deal stage presence she was impetuous and a charismatic speaker. Many thought of her as a saint.

"I know your suffering" she shouted with intense emotion. "We have been used and abused. We have been denied the common entitlement of the working man. We have suffered their indifference and their malfeasance. This is not just a miner's outcry for justice. This is the outcry of the working man throughout Spain who is treated like a mule and made to work in unsafe and unsanitary conditions for a salary that doesn't pay for the bread on his table." The crowd roared their approval after every sentence.

"We have not even been allowed to complain without being victimized by the 'couldn't care less' aristocracy.

It is from our labor, from the sweat of our brows and the calluses of our hands that this country of ours thrives". Some men shouted "Si!, Si!, Si!" and the chant was taken up by the throng and echoed throughout the square. La Pasionaria raised her hands to regain their attention. "We remain at the bottom of the ladder, upholding the freeloaders on top who wallow in luxury under the protection of the government without the slightest concern for the welfare of the workers and their families." Another roar of approval cut across the plaza. The policemen were nervous. Their horses neighed and shuffled in place. "Our frustration is beyond measure. Our anger is great. There is strength in unity. We can no longer be silent. We can no longer be passive. Now is not the time to wait. Now is not the time to wail. Now is the time to act." The crowd howled and whistled and cheered.

She spoke passionately for hours to the men assembled in the Plaza and incited them to strike. The Police all around were wary. They were there to break up the crowd but there were too few officers of the law for the thousands assembled there. There was nothing to do. But they took note of Dolores Ibárruri's popular appeal and knew she had to be silenced.

The strike that followed promptly turned into an armed insurrection. The Guardia Civil was merciless in their attempt to bring the strikers in line. They had no qualms about shooting at random into the crowd. Bodies were lying all over the place and the strikers retreated, stumbling over those who had been shot and determined to seek revenge.

The miners were poorly equipped and had few arms. But they were adept in the use of dynamite and they used it effectively. The dynamiters came on smoking cigars with which they lit the sticks grasped in their hands and threw them at the Civil Guard. The battle that followed made all the newspapers with photos of the carnage and students and factory workers in many cities throughout Spain joined the fray. There were riots on university campuses, strikes and sit-ins in factories and blackouts at night in major cities as electrical workers walked out. Spain was in disarray. It took a long time to restore order.

The authorities blamed La Pasionaria for the strike and the violence which ensued and her arrest and riddance were made of the essence. Every arm of the law, the militia, the police, the army, and the Guardia Civil, all were given strict orders that she be brought in or made "to disappear". The policía secreto in civilian clothes combed the entire province and offered money to informers in an effort to nab La Pasionaria.

Dolores Ibárruri was forewarned and went into hiding. Asturias was friendly territory and she was sheltered by one or another in town after town. From one house to the next each of her hosts treated her as an honored guest but no one could keep her for any length of time. The police were in a house-to-house search and something had to be done. At the last Paco and Fuencísla took La Pasionaria into their home and hid her in a room in their basement.

*   *   *

MANÓLO HAD BEEN SLEEPING since noon. He had a recurring dream in which he was swinging his pickax against the rock wall of the damp mine shaft, interrupted now and then by a wracking cough from his coal dust covered lungs. Then the explosion, the cave-in and the wall collapsing on his friends Paco and Estèfan. The screams and the moans of injured miners. His desperate efforts to get his friends out from under the rubble. He turned over in his sleep to shake the black coal out off his dream and pulled himself up the mine shaft breathing deeply and squinting at the bright light of day.

There was a knock on the door and the dream faded. Manólo sat up and looked at his watch. It was four o'clock in the afternoon and he had only slept a few hours. The knock repeated itself and Manólo put on his slippers and went to the door. Two men stood there. The tall one with the bony cheeks and a harried look in his eyes spoke first. "Manólo García?"

Manólo shuddered and the blood ran to his face. "Si Señor". They had found him out. He would be taken to police headquarters and made to talk, tortured to reveal the authors of *La Verdad*. It was the end of the line. Capitàn Salazar had looked straight at him in his accusations. "It comes from one of your barrios. You know everything that goes on in them".

"My name is Julio Machete and this is Ramon Perez, We are from the Workers' Alliance in Asturias." Manólo breathed a sigh of relief and invited them in. Over a vaso de vino they told him the purpose of their visit. The authorities had made it a priority to arrest La Pasionaria and had the secret police in plain clothes comb Mieres and the area around looking for her. The search was intense. She was now hiding in Paco's house and it was no longer safe so Paco had Julio and Ramon bring Dolores Ibárruri to Madrid where "his friend Manólo might be able to help".

It was a major task and a risky one at that but Manólo agreed to take her in and do whatever he could for her. He inquired about Paco and Estèfan's family and they brought him up to date. Then they had another glass of wine, shook hands and left saying they'd be back within the hour. Manólo was perturbed but he knew Miguel would know what to do. His anxiety was overshadowed by his anticipation and the thrill of meeting her again.

Julio Machete and Ramon Perez came back an hour later with La Pasionaria. She wore a mantilla over her head and was carrying a satchel full of books and papers. She removed her shawl and though she had only met him once she greeted Manólo as she would a friend. She expressed her gratitude for his hospitality, especially since it put Manólo at risk. There were so many supporters she was indebted to but she took it in stride. The cause was more important than the people who took part in it. She spent the night on the cot in the kitchen while Manólo walked the streets of his barrio. He was proud to have the woman who had become such an important and controversial person as a guest in his humble abode.

*   *   *

AT 2 A.M. WHEN MOST RESIDENTS were back in their stall Manólo stood in front of Miguel's portal and clapped three times then twice again immediately. It was their code signal and within minutes Miguel came out. They shook hands and embraced and Manólo told him the story.

"You did right" Miguel said. There was no hesitation. Miguel had known about La Pasionaria. She was an icon of the resistance in the battle to rid Spain of the Franco dictatorship. "But I'm worried" he said. "Madrid is not a safe place for Ibárruri. There is too much police activity. The Guardia Civil has been stopping people on the street and asking for identification. Anyone suspicious is arrested and winds up as a political detainee."

"So what will you do?" Manólo asked.

Miguel reflected for a moment. "I think she'll be safer in Catalonia. She has a number of colleagues there."

The next day Miguel came and took Dolores Ibárruri to the railroad station. They boarded the train to Barcelona and, being approximately the same age, they passed for a married couple. During the long ride they shared the food he had brought and talked. Miguel pumped Dolores with questions. He was curious to know how a simple person with little education wound up becoming such a flaming revolutionary. She was the eighth of eleven children and lived in abject squalor. At 20 she married Julián Ruiz a miner and political activist and had six children herself. After his participation in a general strike Ruiz was imprisoned and, seething with anger, she started writing for El Minero Vizcaino, the miners' newspaper. To preserve her identity she wrote under the name of La Pasionaria but now, with her notoriety, her identity had been revealed placing her in great danger.

Miguel told her of his activities and disclosed to her that he was the publisher of *"La Verdad"*, the clandestine underground paper which seemed to be everywhere nowadays and read avidly. Dolores shook her head. "You are leading a double life compadre. A respected university professor by day and a rebel at night."

"I do what I can for the cause. My standing at the university gives me much leeway to spread the message to idealistic and impressionable young men. But I'm not out there like you. The authorities don't know who authors and distributes *La Verdad*. So far I have been able to remain out of the limelight". La Verdad had become marked by the authorities who tried time and time again to locate its source. Just as they were after La Passionaria they were after Miguel and his group.

Barcelona was a bastion of independence and La Pasionaria had many followers there. Miguel dropped her off at one of their lodges and they shook hands, each acknowledging that they were both engaged in the same struggle and wishing each other luck. Miguel was to find out later that she had become the head of the Popular Front.

*   *   *

ON THE TRAIN RIDE BACK to Madrid Miguel noticed the many burned out churches. His conversation with Dolores Ibárruri had taken up all of his attention and he had not noticed it before. There were armed soldiers at every station, broken windows and bombed out houses, and signs *"Abajo con Hitler! Fuera con Fascismo!"* with *"Viva el Rey!"* right next to it. Spain was in an uproar. It was father against son, neighbor against neighbor with horrendous acts of violence and atrocities committed by both sides. Actually there were many sides from fascists, royalists and anarchists to communists, socialists and republicans and in the midst of all this an election was coming up.

CHAPTER 19

THERE WERE JUBILANT DEMONSTRATIONS in Madrid after the Popular Front, a left-wing coalition of which La Pasionaria was the leader, won the elections. The Spanish love to party and Madrilleños jumped at the occasion. There were fireworks from the rooftops of buildings which lit up the Madrid night and guitar and accordion music in every quarter made for dancing in the street.

Those who did not vote for the Popular Front were disgruntled and reacted violently. While the Spaniards made merry and reveled in the street, at a clandestine meeting of the Falange's Blue Shirts members called for drastic measures. After lesser alternatives were discussed it was decided that José Castillo, a protégé of La Pasionaria and an ardent politico who was pushing for popular socialist reforms, would have to be killed. In the stunned silence of those who were reticent Arturo Belandro rose to his feet and volunteered to see that it was done. He picked Juan Lázaro and Armando de la Cruz as his accomplices. Juan was a thug who bordered on the psychotic and loved violence. He really had no political inclinations but he reveled in the respect he received from being the enforcer. Armando was of the nobility "Armando de la Cruz". He had broken with his family and rejected their values to become a down to earth rebel.

He was an expert planner and worked out the details of the assassination.

*   *   *

IT WAS A HOT DAY in the barrio. Manólo sat in the shade of an elm tree that grew out of place in the yard. He was looking at the morning paper and the headline distressed him.

LA PRENSA
Madrid June 13, 1936

José Castillo, a prominent socialist leader, was murdered yesterday by a Falangist gang as he left his home in Madrid. He was peppered with bullets from several directions and was dead on site. Several witnesses came forth with a partial description of the perpetrators. Police Chief Malcom Debria promised a prompt and vigorous inquiry.

Manólo pulled out a kerchief and wiped the back of his neck. Added to the stifling heat was the tension that reigned throughout the neighborhood. The barrio had its share of fascists, royalists, socialists and republicans. A state of latent hostility caused anxiety to the residents and neighbors were distrustful and wary of each other.

When night fell and Manólo took up his route he had a sense of foreboding. Many people, who usually stayed out late, had turned in early. It was as if they were expecting something to happen. And it did. It came on like a wave. A group of young socialist hoods with torches, angry at the assassination of José Castillo, swept though the barrios on a rampage, breaking windows and setting fires. Manólo was helpless and beside himself. The whistle of all the Serenos around blew loud and long but there was nothing they could do by themselves. By the time the police came the gangs had gone through and left a lot of damage. A Molotov cocktail had been hurled into Colonel Belandro's courtyard and the firemen had a time putting it out. Many windows had been broken at the residence of the Grandee Gomez Di Silva. The murder of José Castillo had ignited a fire which had been simmering for a long time. The police were under a lot of public pressure to bring the killers to justice. Police Chief Debria personally interviewed the purported witnesses and thought he was able to make out a number of potential suspects.

LA PRENSA
Madrid, July 10, 1936

Three individuals have been arrested in connection with the assassination of José Castillo, a prominent member of the Socialist party. Juan Lazaro, Armando de la Cruz, and another unnamed accomplice were taken into custody yesterday and held in the local prison . . .

The unnamed accomplice was of course Arturo Belandro. After intensive behind the scene manipulation, Colonel Marcos Belandro succeeded in having Arturo released and removed from the list of suspects. To keep him away from further implication in the murder he sent him out of the country.

*　*　*

ONE THING FOLLOWED ANOTHER in rapid sequence. The right countered with a series of murders and assassinations by fascist gunmen. In reprisal, spontaneously and almost overnight, workers' militias were formed. Workers seized factories and other workplaces. The church, openly pro-fascist, was the subject of much anger and many churches were burned and sacked. The violence escalated and spread throughout the country. Spain was searing. The pot was sure to boil and break into civil war.

Their interests and their ideals threatened, the landed aristocracy, the church, the monarchists, and a large military clique rallied against the government, as did the Falange, a new fascist party led by General Francisco Franco, the Caudillo. After an attempted coup d'état committed by parts of the army against the government the Spanish army and its rebel counterpart confronted each other and the civil war exploded with full force. But it was more than a civil war. Spain became the battle ground, the arena in which socialism and fascism faced off. Both sides were soon receiving aid from abroad. The International Brigades supported Republican Spain. Italy and Germany aided Franco with an abundance of planes, tanks, and other materiel.

* * *

ON JULY 18, 1936 DOLORES IBÁRRURI, La Pasionaria, who had become the head of the Popular Front and was a violent anti-fascist, gave a lengthy radio address to the Spanish people denouncing the Nationalist uprising and inciting them to resist the onslaught of the rebel army. "Better to die on one's feet than to live on one's knees" she entreated and ended her speech with an impassioned shout "The fascists shall not pass! No Pasaran!".

"NO PASARAN!" became the battle cry of the Republicans.

* * *

THE REBEL ARMY WAS LED by a consort of career officers who came from the upper classes and did not support the elected government. They brought their men under the command of General Francisco Franco and looked to him as the "Caudillo" the leader. It seemed like it would never end. Saving the Spanish republic from another dictatorship became the idealistic cause of the era, a cause for which many were fighting. Miguel was among them.

Lying in a trench next to Sammy and Raoul, Miguel lit a cigarette and looked around. There were a few dozen men of all ages sitting on the ground cradling their riffle. They had become close during the weeks of fighting and the loss of one was felt by all the others. They were a ragtag bunch, fervent but untrained and badly equipped. Only Capitàn Gonzales had some experience leading men in battle. Like a number of other officers of the Spanish army, he had dropped from the ranks to join the partisans and was now fighting those with whom he had trained.

On each side of the narrow field there were damp pillboxes which were occupied by opposing forces. It had rained all night and the men were caked with the mud in the trenches. The boots they were wearing were of poor quality and the water soaked right through to their socks. The hardship was great but no one complained. Shultz the German and Santini the Italian were standing guard. Both were anti-fascists who fought alongside the Republicans. Not a shot had been fired in nearly half an hour and the lull was ominous.

Early that morning the cannonade had been intense. At one point Miguel would have been a victim but for a young man named Sendoa who pushed him to the ground just moments before an artillery shell whistled by and exploded in the trench killing two men and wounding three others.

*   *   *

"I NEED FOUR MEN to blow up a train full of ammunition" the Captain shouted and more than twelve men stepped forward, Miguel among them. The Captain pointed to Raoul, Sammy, Miguel and Sendoa.

In semi-darkness they made their way up the embankment and trekked through the mud, Raoul taking the point, assault weapon in hand and eyes on the lookout, Miguel and Sendoa carrying the explosives, and Sammy following with the spool of wire and the detonator. Cautiously they crept over the parapet in an uncanny silence. Sendoa was the only one who had handled explosives before and when they reached the railroad track he directed the placement in the shadow of a water tower where the light of the locomotive would not discern it. Then they all climbed down and crouched in the ditch some 300 feet away and waited in silence. When they could feel the rattle of the train which made the rails vibrate from afar they took up their positions. As the loaded cars rolled by they set off the dynamite. The explosion lit up the sky and fragments showered the landscape, some falling to within a few feet from where the men lay flat on the ground, covering their heads, their ears bursting from the sound. Then they made their way back to report to Capitàn Gonzales only to find that he had suffered a severe wound and been taken to the rear by an orderly.

During the mission, Miguel, Sendoa, Sammy and Raoul had shared fear mixed with a rush of adrenaline, and grown close. When they got back they developed a camaraderie as only companions in arms do.

Sendoa was 24. He was Basque. Brawny and proud he wore the typical Basque beret tilted to the side, a bandoleer with cartridges diagonally across his chest, and worn leather boots up to his knees. The Basques were a special people. They had their own culture, their own music, and even their own language Euskera. They had a great deal of pride in their singularity and had for many years sought to maintain their identity. When the government outlawed the use of their language in the schools, the Basques formed their own councils and took on the government. At first their action was relatively tame but the government responded by imprisoning dissidents and using strong arm techniques to keep the people in line. The police beat and tortured their prisoners and executed thousands without trial. The Euskadis countered by resorting to sabotage, and escalated to terrorism and assassinations. When the civil war broke out Basques saw an opportunity to participate in the overthrow of the oppressive regime and many joined the Republicans and fought alongside of them as Sendoa was doing.

Sammy and Raoul came from Alicante. They were cousins and ardent Republicans. Their units had been decimated and they joined Capitàn Gonzales's company to continue the fight. Now Capitàn Gonzales had been taken to a field hospital and the unit was led by Claudio Artagón a disgruntled Captain who had been on the front lines for a time and had a nine days' growth of beard. He was gruff. In a show of foolhardy bravado he led his men in a virulent attack which was repulsed, inflicting heavy losses. They were peppered by rifles and machine guns and experienced the fiercest barrage. The high-pitched whine of falling shell fragments filled the air. Miguel crouched alongside Armando and Matty who had survived the onslaught. His hearing was deafened by every kind of explosion from the hacking cough of bombs to the metallic clanging of 5.9 shells bursting in echoing volleys.

Captain Artagón felt the weight of the dead and wounded in his company. It wrecked havoc on his psyche. He became disoriented and walked the fosse in a daze, stumbling over the bodies of his men, wounded, dead or dying. Shell-shocked he stood up and looked over the trench and was instantly blown off his feet by the concussion of bursting shells.

*   *   *

THE BATTLES TOOK PLACE over mountain passes that would have given access to Madrid. General José Miaja sent three International Brigades to the Jarama Valley to block the advance. On the 12th of February, at what became known as Suicide Hill, the Republicans suffered heavy casualties.

Despite the aid of the International Brigades and the support of the majority of the Spanish people, a year into the war the government forces were in retreat. The rebel army led by Generalissimo Francisco Franco had run over most of the country and taken the major cities. Pockets of resistance here and there fought on and Madrid remained in Republican hands.

*   *   *

THE FIGHTING HAD BEEN BLOODY and the wounded, the maimed and the dead were beyond count. In many trenches there were mutilated bodies that had not yet found their grave. There was no medic and the wounded lay around unattended. Since his father had been a doctor Miguel had some knowledge of medicine and patched up those he could, putting tourniquets on bleeding men, bandages on others, and taking cover when a volley of machine gun fire sliced the air overhead or a mortar round exploded nearby.

When the guns let up he sat in the trench alongside his comrades, leaning against the side and trying as best he could to catch some sleep. He thought of Manólo and his barrio. Miguel was fond of him. They had spent so many years together there was a powerful bond between them. He somehow felt he was fighting for him as well as for Spain.

Dear Manólo,

The fighting has been fierce but I am well. I hope you are too. Early this morning the cannonade was intense. At one point I would have caught it but for a young man named Sendoa who pushed me to the ground just moments before an artillery shell whistled by and exploded in the next trench killing and wounding several men. If not for him this letter would not have been written. I have seen enough horror to last me a lifetime.

I hope this war ends soon and that I return in one piece. I think of you often, especially at night when I look up at the sky and see you walking the streets of the barrio with the ring of keys around your neck.

Abrazos,
Your friend,
Miguel

THERE WAS A SUDDEN BUZZING IN THE SKY and the men ducked deep into the trenches. Two German planes flew overhead, made several passes dropping bombs then flew low and strafed the men in the trenches. When they had passed there were piercing screams of pain and anguish all around. Miguel didn't know where to turn. There was panic everywhere. Several men ran out of the trenches and were cut down by machine-gun fire from the pillboxes on the other side.

Then another plane flew over and the last thing Miguel heard was the whistling sound of the bomb before it exploded eight feet in front of him.

CHAPTER 20

MADRID WAS A STRONGHOLD of the Republic. Manólo walked his barrio and found the nights more quiet than usual. After the attack on their compound Don Carlos Gomez Di Silva, the Grandee of Spain had fled to France. So had Colonel Marcos Belandro and his family. They joined their son Arturo who had rented a villa on the outskirts of Nice on the French Riviera. Most of the residents were Republicans but there were other fascists in the Barrio as well. They were not many but they were there and they tried to be as inconspicuous as possible so as to avoid confrontations with their neighbors. Few people went out after dark. It seemed as though the Civil War had scared them into their houses and they tried to hide under their blankets.

Manólo had been tempted to join Miguel and the partisans as his Asturian friend Estèfan had done. Paco's leg had never healed properly and he had a limp which prevented him from joining Estèfan in the fight. Manólo also wanted to go but he felt he was needed by his flock in the barrio. It didn't matter to him what their political leanings were. He had been there almost seventeen years. He was the caretaker, the keeper. He felt more important now than he had in the past and the residents accorded him more respect. His was a reassuring presence. He was the Sereno for all of them no matter what their beliefs and as long as he walked the street at night everything would be "serene". They would have slept better if, as had been the case so long ago, the Sereno would call out hourly *"Son las dos y sereno"*.

When the sirens went off startling them awake they came out of their houses in pajamas, house robes and slippers, disheveled and without makeup. Manólo helped them down two flights of stairs in a compound that had a wine cellar and now served as an air raid shelter. Madrillenos who found themselves on the street at this time sought shelter in the Metro. Manólo hung a wet blanket at the entrance to the stairway to protect them from the mustard gas that had been used by the Germans in the first world war. The cellar was damp and imbued with the odor of the wines in barrels that had been stored there for many years. Some thirty people, men, women and children tried to make themselves as comfortable as possible. Some had brought mats, blankets and pillows and the children were their main concern. There was a spirit of cooperation which often happens in times of crisis and it dissolved their differences for the time being. They had no notion how long they'd be there and feared the worst.

In the previous week Hitler's Condor Legions had firebombed Guernica, a place of no military importance, an ancient town of the Basques and the center of their cultural traditions. German Heinkel bombers assailed the town for nearly 4 hours, dropping over 3000 incendiary bombs and reducing it to rubble. As if that was not enough German fighter planes then flew low and machine-gunned civilians who had taken refuge in the fields. There were screams of pain and blood all around. It was a massacre of major proportion. In Paris for the 1937 International Exposition Pablo Picasso painted the wanton atrocity on an enormous canvas as the center piece of the Spanish Pavilion. Radio Nacional, the pro-Franco station made no mention of the bombing of Guernica but the republican station broadcast the slaughter in great detail and the residents in the cellar were in fear of bombs raining down on them.

They huddled together cold and afraid, speaking in whispers, trying to calm the children who sometimes cried filling the cellar with sounds that resonated off the walls and added to everyone's tension. Though the air raid only lasted an hour it seemed a lot longer and when the all-clear sounded there was a collective sigh of relief as they made their way back home knowing they wouldn't sleep the rest of the night.

*   *   *

WHEN MIGUEL CAME TO he was confused. He had been knocked unconscious when the bomb exploded. The fighting had been bitter and there were casualties everywhere. The last thing he remembered was Shultz lying face down in the mud. Now everything was white. He lay on a cot in a make-shift hospital tent with shrapnel wounds to his back and left thigh alongside men who had lost a leg or an arm. Miguel knew that some of them would walk out on crutches while others would be carried out.

"*Como te sientes?*" she said. He heard her as though through a fog. His head had not cleared yet. "*Como te sientes?*" she repeated. Miguel looked up at her. She smiled in her white uniform, leaned over and propped up his pillow. "You'll be alright." she said. Her voice was soft and soothing.

He suddenly thought of his comrades. He raised himself on his elbow. "Raoul?" he asked fearfully. She shook her head from side to side. "Sammy?" he asked. She pointed to a bed to the left and on the far side of the tent. Sammy lay there, a large bandage on his head and over his right eye. "You rest now. I'll be back" she said and walked on. Miguel watched her going from one bed to another, touching and comforting the wounded as best as she could. He shuddered and closed his eyes. He felt pain in his right shoulder but more than that he felt weary and dozed off. Images of the dead, the wounded and the maimed lying in an open field zig-zagged across his dreams. Then the dream changed and the dead and wounded turned into red poppies and Manólo stood in the middle of them holding out his hand.

"*Hola Compañero!*". Miguel half-opened his eyes and saw the hand stretched out to him. Sendoa smiled. "That's twice you almost caught it. I guess the fighting is over for you and you'll be going back to Madrid." Miguel nodded. "That's OK Miguel, I'll continue the good fight for you and when it's over I want you to come and be a guest in my house in Durango. We'll drink sangria and talk over old times". He straightened out his beret, heartily shook Miguel's hand *"Que le vaya bien!"* and walked out.

* * *

IN THE DAYS THAT FOLLOWED the shrapnel in his back gave him much pain but he sought more attention then it called for because he was taken by the nurse who cared for him.

Her name was Yolanda and she came from a small town on the border of Portugal. She risked her life on the battlefield to tend to the fallen. She nursed the wounded, wrote letters from them to their families and helped keep the morale under the tent high. Her misty eyes, her seductive smile and her cascading black hair filled Miguel with emotion. It had been a long time since he had felt this way.

"Este es tuyo?" Yolanda asked opening her hand and showing him a large Egyptian coin.

"Si!" he said without hesitation.

"I found it under your cot" she said. She gave it to him and he clutched Manólo's keepsake in his hand. It seemed as though there was some mystical significance to this exchange. A presage of sorts.

Yolanda was twenty-nine and he was in his late thirties. Despite the weight of his experiences he still had a boyish look. When he could get out of bed she walked with him in the woods behind the camp. He ambled along, leaning on her till they found a log by a stream and sat down. His feelings for her were written all over his face. She reached over and touched his cheek. "My father was a Doctor" Miguel said unexpectedly. "He loved caring for people. When I was a boy he sometimes took me with him when he made house calls. I remember once we went to a boy scout camp in the hills outside Madrid. They had tent setups like here. A boy had fallen off a tree" he rattled on. "He wasn't much older than I and he had a broken leg. It was a clean fracture and my father set it and put it in a plaster cast. He made the plaster right there at the scout camp." Miguel stopped abruptly. "Why am I telling you all this?"

Suddenly a mortar round exploded nearby and they both fell to the ground covering their heads and holding on to each other. The fear of the blast was overshadowed by the warmth and intimacy of the moment. Several more shells exploded some distance away. It had happened before but never so close to a military hospital tent. When the silence returned they sat up and looked around. The sun had come out and fell lightly on the trees and on their shoulders. Everything seemed illuminated and in slow motion. They walked back hand in hand on grass that felt like cotton without saying a word. The war, the mortar, this feeling, it was bitter-sweet and confusing. He shared men he had fought alongside of, with those she had nursed and cared for in their moment of distress.

The next time they sat by the river Miguel put his hand under Yolanda's chin and lifted her head. "I know this is preposterous" he said " . . . but I love you. I really do." She didn't answer but the glitter in her eyes was revealing and in the ten days that she nursed him back to health their love burgeoned. This whirlwind romance in a time of war brought them to a marriage in the field by an army chaplain.

The wedding took place during a surge in the fighting. The field was covered with craters where the bombs had fallen. It was also raining. The rain beat down on the canvas tent and the wind made the roof flap. Miguel had broached Sendoa. "Will you stand for me and be my groomsman?" Sendoa readily agreed. Now he stood alongside Miguel as Father Javier Delgado performed the ceremony. There was Sammy with a patch over his eye and several comrades in arms. It was the field hospital's mess hall only a short distance from the front lines and the service was interrupted now and then by the sound of artillery shells which burst noisily overhead or the whistling of a bomb and the explosion not far off. It was difficult not to wonder how many casualties there were and not to expect that some of them would soon be brought in to the field hospital.

Father Javier Delgado went through the wedding rites with a great deal of emotion. This was a cocoon of love in the midst of violent conflagration. Some men who didn't know the couple stayed and watched just to be where something wholesome and benevolent was happening when there was chaos all around. Miguel was in fatigues and Yolanda in her white nurse's uniform. Unshaken by the lightning and thunder, by the wind and the rain, unshaken by the canon bursts overhead, Miguel and Yolanda looked at each other and exchanged vows. There was love, strength and commitment and though this was not the customary wedding there was no doubt the bridge was solid.

CHAPTER 21

THE NIGHT WAS HOT. Layers of humidity hung in the air. The taxi thread its way through the narrow street and pulled up in front of the residence. Miguel got out first then held out a hand to Yolanda. The cab driver took the suitcases out of the trunk, set them on the ground, collected his fare and drove off.

Miguel looked around dreamily. This is where he had grown up. This is where he had lived. Nothing had changed but it looked different to him. Maybe he was different. He had been in battle. He had seen men bleed. He had seen men die and it would stay with him for the rest of his life.

He turned to Yolanda and she smiled at him. "*Te quiero*" she said and it washed over him and soothed the pain of his thoughts. He took her into his arms and held her there for a long time. Then he drew back put his hands together and clapped twice. He remembered the first time he had done that and this young somewhat clumsy new Sereno had appeared. Miguel was a member of the Academy then and wore the black cape and the orange scarf and he could see from the look on his face that the young Sereno was impressed. Manólo. Manólo. He hadn't known then how deep a friendship would develop between them. Now the clap resonated through the narrow street and there was joy in the anticipation of seeing his old friend. It had been a long time but Miguel knew he was out there somewhere.

Then, out of the darkness, Manólo stumbled and, upon seeing Miguel, his face lit up. They fell into each other's arms and hugged. Miguel recoiled because the shrapnel in his back was still giving him pain. When they broke the embrace he stood holding both of Manólo's hands and they looked at each other in the glow of the street lamp. "This is where we met" they said almost simultaneously. Manólo was elated. The barrio had seemed empty without Miguel. It had been over a year. "It's good to have you back" he said with overflowing emotion.

"It's good to be back". Then, as if he had almost forgotten, he put his arm around Yolanda and brought her in front of him. "Manólo" he said "This is Yolanda, my wife".

Manólo was stunned and stood there wide-eyed. He took off his cap and held out a hand. She took it with both of hers. "I've heard so much about you" she said and there was so much sincerity in her voice. "You must be someone special. Miguel speaks so fondly of you". In a swoop Manólo took her into his heart as if he had been at the wedding and had been the best man. He reached over and kissed her on both cheeks.

"We came from San Sebastian on the 10 O'clock train" Miguel said "but the rails were cut just outside of Burgos and it took three hours to get us going again. The

Falangistas have been active all along the line." Manólo nodded.

Now the lights of the house were on again and they were, for Manólo, like the bright sky he remembered seeing when he looked up the shaft in the elevator cage that hoisted him and his fellow miners to ground level.

* * *

MIGUEL AND YOLANDA had barely settled in. She was in effect his war bride and the war was still raging. The radio blared away as Fernando Valera, a Republican deputy, roused the people:

"Here in Madrid we make a stand for liberty. It is here that we undertake the great struggle, a struggle between 'tyranny and democracy', 'fascism and liberty'. We are fighting for Spain with the mantle of our blood. Madrid! Madrid! Viva la libertad! Viva España! Viva Madrid!"

The war had been on for almost three years and Madrid was the last holdout. To take Madrid General Francisco Franco gave orders for the road that linked the city to the rest of Republican Spain be cut. The fascists took Mount Garibitas, the highest point in the area and shelled the city from on high.

In the barrio at the Iglesia de la Madonna few of the faithful were in attendance. The ones that were, kneeled and prayed fervently as the shells could be heard falling on houses some distance away and bricks and cobblestones flew all over breaking windows and wrecking havoc. There was no way of knowing how this would all end.

Madrid was under siege. Miles of trenches surrounded the city. At the end of the communicating trenches came the actual defense lines, dug within a few feet of the enemy's trenches. At night the Fascist artillery would open up. People of all ages organized into militias based on political affiliation and dug in as best they could. Men with battlefield experience were placed at key points. Barricades were thrown up across Madrid's streets in anticipation of fighting in the city itself and fighting there was, violent street fighting.

* * *

IN THE CENTER OF THE CITY, where the fighting had not yet reached, the cafés were filled with a different kind of people, journalists, state employees, and all sorts of intelligentsia. Armed militia men dressed in monos, the new dark blue uniforms, marched through the streets to the front lines. Most striking to see were workers in their ordinary civilian clothes with rifles over their shoulder.

At La Perla, a restaurant much frequented by locals, there was music and laughter, dancing and rejoicing.

With so much sadness all around there was need for some joy. Pépita and Dulcinea, friends of Yolanda, made her and Miguel a wedding party amid the chaos and the fighting. There was Adolfo and Simón, Pastor and Bernardo and their wives, and Sammy with a patch over the eye he had lost. There were also several of Miguel's students from the University. And there was Manólo who remembered his own wedding in Asturias so many years ago. His had been under less than normal circumstances as well.

Yolanda looked beautiful in her red velvet dress. She had not had a proper wedding and with the lace mantilla over her head she now looked like a bride. Miguel pried Manólo into dancing with her while he sat at the flower covered table and looked at them both with much love and emotion. He knew that by nine o'clock Manólo would have to excuse himself to go and walk the streets of his barrio.

When the band stopped playing, a guitar and an accordion struck up the melody of La Sevillana and they all formed a circle and clapped. Then Pépita, who was from Sevilla and had a flamenco dance studio, stepped into the center and started to tap. She was in her thirties and her slightest movements were graceful and deliberate. She stamped her feet and clapped her hands and moved around in rhythm. Then three women with flowers in their hair entered the dance. They had castanets in their hands and the four of them formed a square and tapped and sang. The dances were joyful and the tables rattled.

They had earlier manifested their fear but this was a wedding party and life carried on. They ate and drank and danced and rejoiced very much aware of the fighting on the other side of the city and trying to forget for a brief moment the carnage that was going on all around them.

*   *   *

THE REBELS HAD BROKEN the Republican line and entered the city. In the streets of Madrid there was a civil war within the Civil War. People who were caught on the "wrong" side of the lines were shot. Probably the most famous of these was the poet and dramatist Federico García Lorca who had been part of the Tertulia, the gathering of poets which met at La Pluma on the Plaza San Ramón in Manólo's barrio when Manólo was the new Sereno. He was labeled a traitor and shot execution style. In addition the war provided an excuse for settling accounts and resolving long-standing feuds. In most areas, even within a single given village, both sides committed atrocities.

As four of his army columns moved on Madrid, fascist General Emilio Mola in a radio address referred to his militant supporters in the capital as his "fifth column". These pro-fascists in Madrid clandestinely undermined the Republican government from within.

In church the faithful were now joined by the fearful. They flocked to the church to pray to Jesus the savior to save them from their fellow countrymen who often went on a rampage and killed at random, combatants and non-combatants, making casualties of women and children who huddled together in fear.

It was a cold February morning. Miguel and Pastor had joined several dozen Madrillenos who, with government forces, manned the barricades. They had turned over several cars and built a wall with cobblestones. Segismundo Casado, commander of the Republican Army, was growing increasingly unhappy by the large number of his soldiers being killed. He was also aware that many ministers, who were talking about the need to fight to the bitter end, were themselves quietly preparing to leave the country. The Republican soldiers still left alive were no longer willing to fight. That left a handful of students and a few dozen workers to confront the enemy.

There was a rumble down the street then a tank came to smash the barricade. Grenades were thrown and missed their mark. Miguel still felt the shrapnel in his back. Not all of it had been taken out and it restrained the motion of his right arm. The government forces fell back in front of the better trained and equipped fascist army and the defense of Madrid crumbled under the onslaught.

CHAPTER 22

THE WAR WAS OVER.

Within days of the fall of Madrid the Falange took charge of all the functions of government and reinforced its hold on the city by giving the police carte blanche. Now any resistance to those who had been rebels became a resistance to the regime and Franco began a reign of terror aimed at the physical liquidation of all his potential enemies. Although the army was divided, the police were fascists or fascist sympathizers and when they were given unbridled authority they didn't have to be told what to do.

A squad of five policemen came down the Calle d'Oro and through an open portal, pushing the portera aside. Within minutes they came out dragging Marco Costenza, disheveled and in handcuffs. They threw him into their paddy wagon with an unrivaled viciousness. He had been a close companion of Dolores Ibárruri, La Pasionaria. He was taken to the countryside and summarily executed. The same scenario repeated itself time after time till some went into hiding and others trembled for fear of being falsely accused of sedition.

Miguel and his comrades had amassed weapons of all sorts and needed a place to hide them. As far as they were concerned the war was not over. It just changed from overt to covert action. They continued their normal daytime activities so as to avert suspicion and made it a point never to be seen together. Miguel knew there were others working toward the same goal all over Spain.

The University had been almost destroyed by shell fire during the earlier and most bitter fighting of the war but now makeshift classrooms and lecture halls had been set up to allow students to return. Miguel went back to teaching. When speaking before an assembly or chatting with a group of students on the lawn he found the opportunity to discreetly spread the message he was printing in *"La Verdad"*.

*   *   *

WHEN YOLANDA TOLD MIGUEL she was pregnant he was jubilant. He had long given up hope of having children. She was beautiful in pregnancy radiating a happiness he shared and he loved her all the more. He was at her beck and call, indulging her cravings and bringing her leechy nuts and pomegranates at various times of day, treating her as if she was fragile and about to break. The thrill of anticipation helped him forget the horrors of war he had seen in the trenches which were still giving him nightmares.

Manólo followed the swelling of Yolanda's belly with apprehension and anxiety. He had not forgotten how his beloved Marie-Carmen's pregnancy had ended. He had not been there to share her glee and give her support as she carried his unborn child. Though much time had passed he still had pangs of guilt about it. The feelings of sadness and longing which had persisted for years and now gave way to fear for Yolanda.

As the months went by and she grew bigger, he ran errands for her and helped her carry her groceries when Miguel was at the University. At night, when he walked the deserted streets after hours, he remembered how he had played games with the cobblestones so many years ago "It's a boy. It's a girl. It's a boy. It's a girl." It was almost as though he was the expectant father and Yolanda was part of his dreams.

* * *

May 20, 1940
3:30 AM

THE SCREAMS WERE LOUD and resonated through the barrio. It was a woman's screams and it came from Miguel's house. Manólo knew Miguel was away at a conference in Toledo and Yolanda wasn't due for several weeks yet. Still to Manólo her screams were Marie-Carmen's screams and a sudden fear gripped him.

Since Dr. Arroyo had moved to Sevilla no one had come to take his place and the nearest physician was a distance away. Manólo found himself knocking hard on Ofelia's door. La Gorda had called upon her skills at times to abort an unwanted pregnancy but she was also a midwife and a healer. She was of gypsy stock. She had come from Zaragoza and delivered more babies than she could count.

They hurried to Yolanda's bedside where she was writhing from the pain of her contractions. Her water had broken and she was lying on soaked sheets. Ofelia quickly changed them and dried her off. Manólo held her hand and squeezed it at every contraction and the scream that went along with it went right through him. There was a sudden flash of lightning followed by thunder and the rain came pouring down. The thunder repeated loud and furious and the lights went out. Manólo quickly lit a number of candles. It was a long night during which Manólo relived the loss of his beloved Marie-Carmen and the son that was stillborn. In between contractions Yolanda smiled at Manólo. She knew what had happened to Manólo's wife and son and sought to relieve his anxiety. "I am fine Manólo. It will be alright. I'm glad you're with me tonight." She looked at him gratefully and affectionately and he responded in kind. He had no words.

With the thunderstorm raging outside and the midwife and Manólo huddled around her Yolanda was in labor for many hours. It was almost dawn when, with Manólo supporting her from behind and Ofelia guiding the birth, Yolanda's screams were replaced by the screams of a healthy baby boy.

Ofelia sponged the baby and handed it to Manólo who held the 'miracle' in his hands for a moment before putting the baby in Yolanda's arms. He felt a healing wash over him, a healing that gave him relief from the pain he had been carrying without knowing it for so many years.

They named the boy Rafael, Rafa for short.

*   *   *

Miguel and Yolanda Arroyo
have the pleasure of inviting you to attend
the christening of their newborn son Rafael
born May 20, 1940.
The baptismal will take place
at the Iglesia de la Madonna
on Sunday at 10 A.M.

IT WAS A BEAUTIFUL SUNDAY MORNING. There were almost two dozen people in the Iglesia de la Madonna. Some were friends. Some were colleagues. Some were students. Then there were a number of women who regularly attended church on Sunday and were delighted to be part of a blessed sacrament. Miguel stood by the baptismal font with Yolanda by his side holding the baby. None of Miguel's cohorts were in attendance. It would have aroused suspicion.

When Manólo arrived he stood alone under the entrance archway and felt a deep emotional stirring within himself. Miguel spotted him and walked over putting his hand on Manólo's shoulder. He looked at him then over to Yolanda with the baby in her arms. "Manólo, you were there when I couldn't be. I will always be grateful to you for that. I want you to be the baby's Godfather". Manólo's eyes glazed over. "I don't know what to say Miguel. I am humbled and honored to have your son as my Godchild. It is a great gift you are making me" he stammered.

Father Eduardo Delmar was conducting the mass with the Eucharistic sequence of morning prayers in Latin. Miguel had a great deal of antipathy toward Father Delmar. He had taken over the ministry when Father Antonio Suarez had a stroke several years back. He was a rather rotund individual with a pleasant demeanor but then he invoked God's blessing on *"Dux Noster Franciscus"*, our Caudillo Franco, at the conclusion of every service and that made Miguel angry. He knew the blessing didn't come from the heart. Spain's Cardinal Primate had decreed that all Priests shall end their service with that blessing. Still he felt a certain undefined bitterness toward him. But this was not a day for resentment. This was a day for rejoicing.

Father Delmar walked over from the sanctuary, took the baby in his arms and, invoking God's Spirit, blessed the child with the Holy water on his forehead, then anointed him with consecrated oil "in the name of the Father, the Son, and the Holy Ghost". Then with the child in his arms he walked through the entire sanctuary, welcoming and introducing the child to the household of God. As he headed down the aisle he looked into the tearful eyes of Señora Vasquez, a church member who had recently confessed her anguish at not being able to have children.

When he finished his round and came back to the font Father Delmar raised the child over his head and offered thanksgiving to God, then gave the baby to unbelieving Miguel who in turn placed the baby in Manólo's hands and they smiled at each other. Manólo held the precious child and knew that he would be part of his life for many years to come. After a while he gave the baby over to Yolanda and got on his knees and prayed. It was something he hadn't done in a long time. He asked God to watch over Rafael and thanked him for Miguel's friendship which was at the very core of his life.

CHAPTER 23

AS SPAIN DID NOT PARTICIPATE in World War I it did not participate in World War II. But between both wars Spain had its own and a great many casualties. It could be seen all over Spain. The horror of the war had left many without an arm or a leg and men sat up against a wall on the sidewalk with a cap in front of them waiting for a handout. Hollow-eyed women in mourning and women who looked out of blank, uncomprehending eyes walked the street as in a daze.

While the rich, who had spent the Civil War in Biarritz and Monte Carlo, now lived in Madrid at the Palace Hotel or the Ritz and ate game, fish, fowl or meat and listened to good swing bands, for the poor everything was rationed, two small rolls made of flour mixed with sawdust, one egg per person per week, and rancid olive oil to cook whatever they could get hold of on the black market. Men would scrounge under the tables of cafés for cigarette butts.

As though they had synchronized their return, the Grandee and the Colonel came back to their residence in the barrio within days of each other. World War II had started and when France fell in the blitzkrieg under the heels of the German army they knew they would be safer in Spain with the Falange in power. They came back pompous and arrogant and looked upon their neighbors with disdain.

Upon his return from exile the Grandee felt the need to celebrate the re-establishment of his presence in Madrid under a right wing government which was supportive of the nobility. Bright lanterns were lit in the courtyard. Attendants in formal attire stood straight at the entrance as horse carriages and fancy cars brought the creme of society to the event. Upper echelon officers with medals and decorations hanging from their dress uniforms and high level government officials in tuxedoes with wives in evening gowns all filed into the reception hall which had been decked out for a banquet. A long table under crystal chandeliers, set with abundance for what could be royalty, with a manservant for every guest, established the triumphant return of Don Carlos Gomez Di Silva, Grandee of Spain. The Grandee raised a toast "to Madrid, to España, and" with the fading portrait of Franco decked out in his martial best in back of him, "to our valiant Caudillo Francisco Franco". Everyone cheered.

Colonel Belandro then proudly announced that his son Arturo had joined the Blue Division that Franco had sent off to fight in Hitler's Wehrmacht on the Russian front. The guests showed their approval by vigorous applause and Emilio Sincero, the Bishop of the diocese offered a prayer for his safe return. After a sumptuous meal the guests assembled in the drawing room where a guitarist gave a recital of the music of Isaac Albéniz.

Suddenly an explosion rocked the compound throwing people to the floor under chandeliers and falling plaster from the ceiling. Panic ensued. Tuxedoes and gowns were stained with blood and people stumbled over each other in an effort to get outside.

Manólo, three cuadras away, heard the loud and violent blast and felt the ground shake under his feet. Frightened residents came to the windows expecting to have to go down to the air raid shelter as they had so many times before. Two young men in berets with satchels on shoulder straps ran down the street and Manólo immediately connected them with whatever was going on so he set out in pursuit. Knowing all the back alleys he cut one off at the lovers' square and held him up against the wall at the point of his chuzo.

The young man with a square jaw and a determined look on his face didn't seem frightened. "Sereno" he said with aplomb "do you know a man named Arroyo . . . Miguel Arroyo?"

Manólo was dumfounded. "Why do you ask?"

"I'm a friend of his. My name is Sendoa. We fought together in the war. I know he lives in this barrio." Manólo looked at the man and believed him. Miguel had vaguely talked about someone with a Basque name like that.

Matéo Guzman came running up panting. "I see you got one" he huffed "*Bueno! Bueno!* I went after the other one but he got away".

Manólo nodded. "The police will be here soon. I'll hold this one till they come. Go see what you can do to help the people who are injured". Matéo turned and ran back to the Grandee's compound. The piercing shrill of ambulance sirens filled the night.

*   *   *

WHEN GUZMAN DISAPPEARED around the corner Manólo walked the perpetrator to Miguel's portal and clapped three times then twice again. Miguel came out and, upon seeing Sendoa, quickly pulled him and Manólo inside and closed the portal.

"Sendoa, what are you doing here? I heard the explosion. Did you . . . ?"

"Yes. They think the war is over but it isn't. It has just begun."

"Why? Hasn't there been enough killing?"

Sendoa shook his head. "That compound held many of the men who committed atrocities during the war and are still committing them today. Perhaps not in Madrid but up north in Euskadi. They are putting hundreds of

186

thousands of people in prison and executing many of them without a trial. My brother Enrique was shot with three others in the main square in Durango. We were made to watch the execution". Sendoa almost lost his composure. "Mamà Irune has been desolate and hasn't stopped crying since".

Yolanda had heard the eruption and tried to calm the baby who was crying in his crib. When she heard the commotion in the courtyard she came down with the baby in her arms. "I know you" she said looking at him wide-eyed. "I forgot your name but I remember you stood in at our wedding".

"Sendoa". He bowed, took her hand and kissed it. "And now a baby. *Felicitación*".

"It's a boy. His name is Rafael".

"A good name. I'm happy for the two of you. I wish we could have come together under more pleasant circumstances but we're still under the sledge hammer. They're trying to enforce laws that compel us to ignore our Basque language and our culture and they're going about it with a brutality that is beyond measure, rape, torture, indiscriminate killings". The smile left his face. Sendoa was a firebrand, an ardent Basque right down to his soul. "They have stolen our identity and we are going to take it back at any price. You and the rest of Spain are going to benefit from it because we are going to rid you of this malevolent dictator".

"That's not the way to do things" Miguel interjected.

"What other way is there? They have the power, the guns, and they're not hesitant to use it".

Manólo stood there, torn between having to turn this man in and accepting him as a friend of Miguel's. As if Miguel could read Manólo's dilemma he turned to him. "Manólo, this man saved my life".

"These fascists must be stopped" Sendoa continued. "There were six of us here and we're risking our lives working for the same cause. We can't just stand idly by."

"But violence? You must know that I have been putting out an underground paper called *"La Verdad"* and I've gone back to printing and distributing it far and wide. The old saying still goes 'The pen is mightier than the sword'.

"YOU are *'La Verdad'*?"

"Well, I'm not alone. There are a few of us working on it."

"They've been after you for a long time. I guess we're on the same side of the fight again. You have to come up to Euskadi and see what's happening up there. You might find that violence is justified."

A loud rap on the door brought the conversation to an end. Miguel shooed Sendoa into a dark corner of the court yard and brought Yolanda and the baby out of the shadow. Manólo opened the portal to three members of the Guardia Civil with rifles on their shoulders.

"Have you seen or heard anything suspicious?" asked the sergeant.

"I'm the Sereno of this barrio and I've been going around checking each house. So far . . . nothing."

The sergeant noticed the woman with the child in her arms, and apologized for the disruption. Manólo turned to Miguel and Yolanda as their Sereno. *"Gracias Señor y Señora. Buenas noches"* and walked out with the officers.

*   *   *

LA PRENSA
February 21, 1942

An explosion took place at the residence of Don Carlos Gomez Di Silva while he was entertaining important guests. A number of them were injured but no one was killed. The compound was severely damaged and the Grandee had to move to a hotel till repairs are made. No one has claimed responsibility for this terrible attack."

IT STRUCK THE RULING CLASS like a whip. They had settled in and felt at ease with the new regime. They had taken to resume their life of luxury and indulgence and this incident put them on notice that things would not be the same. After all the Spanish people had elected a legitimate government and fought with their blood to preserve it and prevent the military coup which put Generalissimo Francisco Franco in power.

Since the end of the civil war Franco had proceeded to consolidate his reign by violently squashing all opposition. Dissidents were sought out, arrested and disappeared. Others were imprisoned or shot outright. The attack on the Grandee's residence was a clear indication that there was an underground which would fight to re-establish a legitimate government and would use any means to do so. There would be violence.

CHAPTER 24

MANÓLO WOKE UP to gusts of strong wind hitting the door as if to blow it open. He got up, got dressed and made his way as best he could to Miguel's house. It was Rafa's birthday. He was two and Manólo had bought him a set of wooden alphabet blocks which he carried in a box under his arm. The Levante was blowing in from the south with such force that people were swept along with the garbage on the street which collected in doorways for a brief moment before being swept further on. He was downwind and walked leaning into it closing his eyes often to avoid the hits of pieces of debris that was blowing with it.

In the court yard there were letters strewn about, letters the mailman had neatly piled by the portera's door but which had flown all over like confetti. Manólo picked them up and stacked them under the portera's heavy mat. He noticed a letter addressed to Professor Miguel Arroyo and took it from the pile then climbed the stairs and knocked. Yolanda opened the door carrying young Rafa. He had been crying but the moment he saw Manólo he smiled and stretched his arms toward him. Manólo took him from Yolanda and lifted him high over his head then twirled him around with Rafa giggling and shouting "Tata . . . Tata".

"You're the only one that can make him laugh like that Manólo".

"Happy birthday Rafa" Manólo said reaching for the package he had set down and handing it to the boy.

"You remembered" Yolanda said and kissed him on the cheek.

"How could I forget? I was there".

"You were a great comfort to me Manólo. Although I tried to keep you from worrying I wasn't exactly unconcerned. The baby wasn't expected for several weeks yet and I was totally unprepared". Manólo had strong feelings for Yolanda, feelings he couldn't exactly put his fingers on, perhaps vicarious feelings of love.

"Tata, Tata look!" Rafa shouted with glee. He was sitting on the floor and had made a rickety pyramid with the alphabet blocks. He looked to Manólo as an uncle and called him Tata. Manólo bent down and tousled his black curly hair.

"Oh! I almost forgot. There was a letter for Miguel by the portera's door." He reached in his side pocket, pulled out the envelope and handed it to her.

"Miguel is not at the University today. He left this morning for Granada. He said it was for a teachers' conference but I know better. He's probably meeting with other dissidents who will likely help distribute La Verdad in other parts of Spain.

"You know about La Verdad?".

"I've known for a long time Manólo. We don't talk about it but I know and I'm constantly worried that he'll be found out. Not only will he lose his post at the University but they'll arrest him and try him for treason. I fear for his life".

"I know Yolanda. I've known Miguel since he was 18 and he was a rebel already. He is an incurable idealist and I think he'll remain one for the rest of his life. Well are you going to open it?"

"I don't open Miguel's mail Manólo."

"How long will he be gone?"

"A little over a week."

"You'd better open it then. It might be important."

Yolanda reached for a letter opener on the desk and slit the envelope open. It was from someone named Xisto Marquez:

> *"I hope this letter reaches you in time. The teachers' conference in Granada has been noted by the authorities as a potential meeting ground for dissidents. They have*

infiltrated the members and you should be
very careful who you talk to. Be well my friend.
Viva España".

Yolanda was shaken. There was no way she could reach Miguel to warn him and she knew she would go through mental anguish till he returned. She counted on Manólo to sustain her in times like these.

* * *

THE UNIVERSITY OF GRANADA was a sprawling complex of buildings and the teachers' conference took place in the Blue Room. Some forty teachers came from all over Spain to discuss the new curriculum. The primary focus of their attention was the new Spanish history books which had been mandated by the state and turned the heroes of the civil war into villains and made Francisco Franco into a Napoleonic figure that saved the Spanish nation from chaos.

Most of the teachers who took the podium praised the change and one could assume that the room was full of right-wing supporters of the regime but many of them had simply decided to keep quiet, not daring to speak up, not even to each other for fear of retribution.

During the morning break Miguel gathered with several comrades in the lounge. He knew most of them. It wasn't clear how they all joined in the same spirit of reluctance to accept the mandate of the government. Something indefinable had brought a number of them together and they sat in groups of three or four and talked about ways of getting around the imperative. The lounge was buzzing.

Miguel's objective went much further. He looked around the room and tried to identify some who might be willing to go beyond verbal resistance. His eyes fell on Señor Adam Carmelitano a professor at the University of Valencia, a tall lanky man with the wrinkled suit of an intellectual. Miguel had known him for some time and knew him to be a staunch opponent of the regime. They sat and talked and were joined by Samuel Uribé who introduced himself as associate professor of Humanities at the University of Salamanca. The contrast between him and Carmelitano could not be greater. Uribé was small and bent over and looked more like an accountant than a college professor.

When the conference broke for lunch a rumor went around that the conference had been infiltrated. A science teacher from Salamanca said he had never seen Samuel Uribé on campus and the suspicion spread throughout the room so that Uribé was not included in most conversations which could be labeled treasonous under the government's loose definition of the word. Some others' credentials were scrutinized and many teachers were wary of speaking out when in the presence of someone they weren't absolutely sure of. Still Uribé could be seen going from one group to another listening

in on conversations which took a different turn the
moment he appeared.

Despite the uneasiness this created, Miguel was able to
secure members of the faculty of four Universities to take
on the distribution of La Verdad in their areas of concern.
This was more than he had hoped for and he took the train
back to Madrid with a sense of accomplishment.

CHAPTER 25

DON MARTÍN DE LAS CASAS did not like being kept waiting. He was a member of the aristocracy and carried himself as such. He was used to having people attend to him rapidly. He was sitting on a bench in front of the office of Don Celestino Menendez, Dean of the University, tugging impatiently at his lapel. When he was shown in, Don Celestino stood behind an elaborately carved wooden desk, a Toulouse Lautrec caricature of a man who, despite his stature, had the respect of most of the faculty. Don Martín de las Casas' greeting to Don Celestino was less than courteous. He shook his hand and sat down across the desk from him with annoyance.

"You look perturbed Don Martín."

"I am very perturbed Don Celestino. My son Alberto has been telling me that his political science professor is a Communist. He spouts left-wing propaganda and tries to inculcate the young minds of the students with his radical ideas."

"Professor Arroyo?"

"I believe that's his name."

"Professor Arroyo is very popular with his students he . . ."

"I don't care how popular he is. I want you to do something about it."

"I'll try Don Martín. I'll talk to him."

"Don't try! Do it!" Don Martín got up to leave. "If you don't I will go to the trustees with my complaint. I see several of them at El Club de la Bandera."

The conversation was abrupt and Don Martín walked out without closing the door. Don Celestino was left standing behind his desk looking rather small for such an impressive office.

* * *

MIGUEL ARROYO was shown into the Dean's office and they exchanged respectful greetings.

"I've had a visit from Don Martín de las Casas yesterday and he's not happy with your teachings of his son Andreas."

"I think Andreas is a very bright student. He adds life to the class, always bringing in the other side of an argument."

"He says you teach Communism." Miguel shook his head. His teachings were radical. In some way they *were* meant to help mold a political belief in his students. "He says you teach Communism" Don Celestino repeated.

Miguel nodded. "Of course Don Celestino. Of course I teach Communism. I teach Communism, and Socialism, and Fascism. They are all political systems. *It is* a political science class."

The expression on Don Celestino's face changed from one of accusation to one of understanding. It made sense of course. "Be a little less impassionate Dr. Arroyo. Perhaps a little less outspoken. Thank you for coming in" and he reached over and shook Miguel's hand.

*   *   *

A MAJOR STRIKE by the Electrical Workers' Union left much of Madrid in the dark. The lights were out everywhere. On Madrid's Gran Via neon-lit theaters darkened and shop windows went black.

In the Barrio Viejo people stumbled through the darkness. Manólo was on familiar ground. He had walked the length and breadth of the barrio so many times that he could do it blindly. The residents were calling for him here and there and he scuttered to lead them home with the flashlight he didn't need for himself.

From the many residences there were candles glowing in the windows giving off warmth and making the area look festive.

At four in the morning Manólo turned unto the Calle Comercial and spotted a bright red light in front of Señor Valparo's bakery some distance ahead. He made his way over there and came upon two vandals. The one was holding a torch while the other took several loaves of bread and sacs of flour through the broken window.

The moment they spotted Manólo they took what they could and ran. The shorter one stumbled and dropped the torch. Manólo hesitated. "Do I stop and extinguish the fire or do I go after them?" He didn't think he'd have much of a problem catching up with them. He had an advantage in the dark. But he thought "loaves of bread, loaves of bread". There's still hunger in the Barrio. He reached down and picked up the torch which was still flaming, took it to the water fountain in the middle of the Plaza and doused it.

*   *   *

ALTHOUGH PROSTITUTION HAD BEEN ILLEGAL for a long time it was tolerated. The police looked the other way and some members often took turns in the beds. But now the orders came down from Franco himself to clamp down on the ladies of the night whether in the streets or in the brothels.

The buzzer rang loud and long. It rang throughout La Gorda's establishment. Although it was still called La Gorda's, Isabella Morros had taken back her name, given up the trade, and retired to a life of leisure on the Isle of Ibíza.

The brothel was now run by Spanish Kate who was not Spanish and whose real name was a mystery. She was a big lady with straw blond hair and big breasts and the look of someone who wouldn't let anyone take advantage of her. She had come from Amsterdam where she had worked the red-light district until the police went after her for beating up a john who was abusing her. She worked at La Gorda's for two years before taking over when Isabella Morros retired.

There were six girls working there now. Sedonia, Mikaela, a Swede they called Yorgensen, and two Italian ladies Sofia and Lucy. It was a busy night and all the girls were servicing their customers. Yorgensen worked the street on the square and acted as a lookout. A grateful client had rigged up a buzzer discreetly behind the phone booth.

As the buzzer rang there was an immediate rush of activities. Although it had never happened before it seemed as though they had rehearsed it. Like the drills when the siren went off during the civil war. The ladies quickly got dressed and helped their johns into their pants. Then they all rushed down a staircase to the cellar and gathered in front of a bolted door.

The men eyed each other on the sly with curiosity and embarrassment at the same time. Moments later Malcom came with the key and unbolted the door. There was a small staircase and a vertical ladder leading down to the narrow ledge of the sewer and they all filed down clumsily. The air was cold, damp and malodorous. Malcom led them with a flashlight several impossibly long cuadras along the skimpy ledge to a metal ladder which exited into the street through a manhole. No sooner were they out that they scrambled in all directions, pulling their hats down or covering their faces with a newspaper.

Meanwhile, back in the drawing room the ashtrays had been cleaned and the pillows straightened. When the police entered with self-aggrandized authority, Spanish Kate was stretched out on the velvet couch with a red blouse, black mesh stockings, and a lot of bright red lipstick, holding a lit cigarette at the end of a holder. Two of the ladies, Sedonia and Mikaela sat on a settee looking in the mirror, while Lucy and Sofia poured themselves a brandy. The detective, in civilian clothes, sent his six uniformed men throughout the house searching for what he knew was no longer there. He waited in the drawing room eyeing the girls and smiling roguishly at Spanish Kate who tried to look seductive despite her age. She reached over and took the bottle and a glass from Sofia.

"Can I offer you a brandy Jeffe?"

The title *"Jeffe"* raised his status by a mile and the detective was perked by the flattery.

"Gracias Señora but I'm on duty. Some other time perhaps" he crooned with a roguish smile. *"Entonces?"* he shouted upstairs.

"Nada!" came the reply.

"Y por abajo?"

"Nadie!"

"Entonces vamonos!"

"My respects Madame" he said bowing to Kate with a glint in his eye. "I am sorry to have inconvenienced you. We have to do our job you know." And they all trooped out into the street. The moment they had gone Kate and the girls burst into laughter and poured each other another brandy.

CHAPTER 26

ALONG MADRID'S GRAN VIA in the early evening, the hour of the *paseo*, smart women in furs and well-dressed men jostle along the avenue, huddled in their mufflers against the chill wind from the Guadarramas. Street lights gleam on the windows of expensive stores and the rickety taxis are always full.

In the cafés crowds jam the tables drinking wine or coffee and eating *tapas*, little plates of grilled shrimp or fried baby octopus tentacles. Silent gray-coated policemen stand discreetly in the background with nothing to do but chase away the beggars who paw at the sleeves of guests exhausted after a night's dancing at the Ritz Gardens.

But on the other side of town the cafés are not so fancy. At the Café Gijón men gather around a marble-topped table and, over endless cups of *cafés solos* tear the regime apart. "*I work at the textile factory. I have the night shift. I have a wife and child and my pay is 14 pesetas a day. How can I feed my family with that?*" griped Manuel. The men all nod and discuss the work stoppages going on throughout the country with the threat of more audacious and aggressive action that was beginning to take place.

It began in the coal fields of Asturias. Miners whose demands had not been met refused to go down the shafts. Though strikes were illegal they stuck to their guns and their tenacity won them sympathizers far and wide. The walkout fanned out into factories and shipyards all over Spain. As usual, the students of the University joined the fray and were at the center of the conflict.

*   *   *

MIGUEL WAS STANDING AT THE PODIUM lecturing to an attentive class when he was interrupted by Maestro Antonio Ferarra Comesaño, head of the political science department who dismissed the class and escorted Miguel to the office of the administration.

Dean Menendez offered Miguel a seat without looking up. He continued thumbing through a file for several minutes, turning pages and making notes. He didn't relish what he was about to do. The time he took before he said a word was meant to prepare.

"Professor Arroyo . . ." he leaned back in his chair "your teachings are unorthodox. They are out of line". He left a space between each phrase as if to allow the meaning of what he was saying to sink in. "They encourage dissension. I've spoken with you before. You have become an embarrassment to the University". He leaned forward and looked directly at Miguel. "I regret to inform you that it has been decided to let you go. I am sorry. You will finish out the week and clean out your desk." Miguel sat there stunned. "That's all! You may go".

*   *   *

IT DIDN'T TAKE LONG for the word to spread throughout the campus. Miguel Arroyo was a beloved teacher and the students were not ready to accept his dismissal. They went on strike staying out of class and demonstrating with placards demanding Miguel's reinstatement. There was so much unrest at the University that many classes were canceled for lack of attendance. Students marched through campus shouting *"REINSTATE PROFESSOR ARROYO! REINSTATE PROFESSOR ARROYO!"*

The administration was nervous and called the police who patrolled the University grounds. One thing led to another. Armed officers slapped their short clubs in the palm of their hand and dared the students to try something. Luis Obrigero one of the student leaders and several of his cronies did not back down. Two policemen grabbed him by the collar and tried to drag him away. That started a riot. The students had been simmering for so long now that their rage erupted. They threw bottles and battled the police with stones, smashed windows and set furniture ablaze.

The army was called in to re-establish order. Armed soldiers surrounded the students on the campus green and when another bottle was thrown they fired into the crowd. A number of student leaders were wounded. Luis

Obrigero was killed. There were screams and students fell all over each other in an attempt to get away.

The next day the walls of Madrid were bleeding, crying, and shouting to the people *"Huelga, Huelga. Todo al funerale de nuestro compañero Luis!"* "Strike, strike, everyone to the funeral of our murdered comrade Luis!"

*   *   *

THERE WAS DISTRESS in the coffee houses. You could feel the tension like a volcano about to erupt. The Guardia Civil stopped every other person and asked for their ID card. If you didn't have any you were in trouble. Blue-shirted Falange strong-arm men had taken to arrest and persecute anyone they suspected of sedition.

Press censorship and government surveillance of potential political leaders restricted dissent across Spain. Police were carrying out orders to seize all copies of newspapers that were known to be insurgent and looking for *La Verdad*, the one that had been a thorn in their side for a long time as it called upon Spaniards to organize into cells to actively oppose the dictatorship.

Miguel made his way home from the University. He had escaped the rampage by cutting across the soccer field. As he came upon the Plaza San Ramón he noticed several men of the secret police. They were obvious with their identical coats and hats. Miguel crossed the Plaza and ducked into the church. The Vespers service was in progress and Miguel allowed himself to be distracted from the certainty that he and his cell were the object of their attention. He remembered how he had been reluctant to attend church with his parents and now that they were gone he wished he had been more indulgent. He crossed himself and walked out the side door. On the other side of the street there were a number of handbills pasted on the wall alongside an official sign which read "POST NO BILLS".

When their printing press had broken down and until it was repaired *La Verdad* had turned to chain letters and clandestine pamphlets. Bright-colored opposition handbills showed up on tables in cafés, on street corners, and plastered on walls and telephone poles.

CHAPTER 27

IN AN ALLEY in back of the Calle Aciago there was a widow they called La Dolorosa. When her husband died at the hands of the secret police she grieved for a long time. Manólo could hear her crying in her sleep at night. On the few occasions when he opened the portal for her he tried to comfort her as best he could and gained her confidence. Alone and lonely in this vast empty space she moved to Salamanca to be close to her family. The compound had now been empty for over two years.

Before she left the widow took Manólo aside. "In back of my court yard there is a locked door" she told him. "A narrow staircase leads to a cellar in which we used to store wine when Xavier was alive. He loved good wine and there are still many bottles of vintage wine there. Enjoy them". And she handed him the key. When Manólo went down to look he thought it would be an ideal place to store the large cache of arms Miguel and his friends had accumulated and was taking up too much space in the print shop. He turned Miguel on to the place and made him a duplicate of the key.

In the wee hours of the morning, under cover of darkness, the cache was moved from Miguel's compound to La Dolorosa's wine cellar. Unlike Sendoa they had no plans for using any guns or explosives at this time. Their purpose was not terrorism or assassination. It was to arouse Spaniards to revolt against Franco's violent regime. While moving the stash of arms they discovered a door nailed shut in back of one of the wine racks. They pried it open and found a vertical shaft with stairs leading lower still. They took a flashlight and went down. It led to a subterranean conduit which carried off sewage and surface water. It was connected and ran all over under the streets of Madrid and many cellars had access to the passage. They pushed a wine rack up against the door to prevent anyone from coming in that way. Little did they know that that door would ultimately become very useful to them.

*　　*　　*

COLONEL BELANDRO had not heard from Arturo for many months and kept looking after the mailman for a letter from his son. But none came. One day in March of 1943 an Italian officer he had known in the first World War came by to tell him that Arturo had been captured by the Soviets and interned in a Russian gulag in the far-flung ends of Siberia. No news would be forthcoming. There were so many stories going around about the cruelty of the Soviets that Colonel Belandro feared the worst. Arturo would be shot or die of starvation. Maybe freeze to death in the bitter cold of the Siberian labor camp. But the Colonel was stoic. It was his code. A man goes to war and takes risks. That was the soldier's lot and a father must remain stalwart and proud. Colonel Marcos Belandro's whole family had been in the military. Throughout the residence there were portraits of his ancestors all dressed in uniforms of various kinds, men who had probably never seen a battle but stood lordly in an arrogant display of power.

His wife Victoria Belandro, who did not share her husband's views and had tried to prevent Arturo from leaving for the Russian front, had eyes that looked like fountains of tears and seemed to be inconsolable. She wore black as if she were already in mourning. She stopped speaking to her husband and blamed him for her loss. Her despondency prevailed until the Summer of 1945 when, to everyone's surprise, the Soviets opened the overcrowded Siberian gulags and released the prisoners.

Arturo came home in mid-August when the heat in Madrid was dry and oppressive but to Arturo it was a welcome relief from the harsh Siberian winter. He was a different person. Three years in the Russian gulag had made him a bitter young man with a pinched face and premature wrinkles. He had also become a staunch anti-communist.

Above ground in the Barrio, that is to say in the daytime, there was animosity in the air. The Barrio was mostly workers, tradesman, and left-wing liberals. The Grandee and the Colonel were among the few staunch fascists. As such they were the target of much malignment and graffiti often appeared on their walls. Because of their high status in the party a number of police officers were assigned to patrol the barrio in the daytime to prevent vandalism. As a side effect the presence of the police made it more difficult for Miguel and his colleagues to pursue their illicit activities.

Below ground, in the mine, that is to say at night, it was all one calm neighborhood with Manólo as its anonymous night watchman.

* * *

AMONG THE NOTABLES of the Barrio Viejo there was an old lady the children called Baba. She had been a portera for many years at a residence on a side street, several cuadras from the Iglesia de la Madonna. It was divided into apartments occupied by four families.

There was Guillermo Calderon a roving banking examiner who traveled constantly around Spain, dropping in unexpectedly on a bank in Zaragossa or Valencia, to the immediate concern and fright of the local bank manager. He was away most of the time and his wife Palma found it difficult to keep her two teenage sons in line. But they lived comfortably and it was rumored that Calderon took payola from bankers not to notice the irregularities in their books. Although there was no proof people suspected him of being a fascist.

There was Marcello an artist with an independent income, who lived alone and spent his days behind an easel in parks and gardens throughout Madrid.

There was Solé and Joaquin, an elderly couple that went out every morning walking slowly hand-in-hand the entire length of the barrio and back without as much as stopping at a café for a drink.

And there was Andrew Summers, an American expatriate who acted as a stringer for the New York Times. He had covered the Civil War and was now writing about the aftermath. During the war he had worked for the Reuters News Agency in London. On the roof he had carrier pigeons which served when the power was out and the telegraph cables weren't operative. When Madrid was surrounded by the Nationalist forces and there was no means of communicating with the outside world Summers used his carrier pigeons to send his news to Reuters. Baba took pleasure going on the roof to feed his pigeons.

When Baba could no longer do her job and had to surrender her lodgings by the portal's entrance to a young couple, the residents agreed to let Baba stay on. She lived in the back in a small unit, one room dark and dreary, with a kitchen alcove and a toilet under the stairwell. In winter she warmed herself and cooked on a cast iron stove that burned coal, coal that she had to stand in line for and often couldn't afford. She was a lovely old woman, always dressed in black, with her gray hair tied in a bun.

She had become a favorite in the Barrio and looked upon as the Barrio's mascot. She was particularly popular with the young mothers who often asked her to take their little ones to the park. On any sunny afternoon she could be seen wheeling a pram or sitting on a bench knitting, with a watchful eye on a toddler or two playing in the sandbox, or rocking the baby in his carriage.

Rafa loved her. He was four and a mischievous boy. He looked forward to teasing Baba by coming up behind her and pulling the stick that held her bun together or hiding behind a tree. Often he would pretend to have fallen so she would pick him up and hold him in her arms. He would snuggle up against her for warmth, comfort and affection. She cuddled him in his early years, told him stories and watched him as he grew up.

At twelve he was tall and hardy and tops in his class without even trying. There were four people in his young life his mother Yolanda who was beautiful and whom he adored, his father Miguel whom he looked up to and respected greatly, Manólo his Godfather whom he thought of as an uncle, and Baba the sweet old lady who had sheltered him and of whom he felt protective now. He frequently went to her lodge after school to make sure she was alright. She always welcomed him with a cup of hot tea and some biscuits. He would sit with her and she would start with "Have I told you about the time when . . ." And Rafa would listen as she told him stories of her life and float dreamily into nostalgia.

As she got older and things became more difficult for her, Rafa walked her to the playground and sat her down on a bench to watch the new generation of toddlers at play. Often Rafa brought her oil for her lamps and some fresh vegetables when he could borrow the money from his father.

*　　*　　*

THE WINTER OF 1954 was brutal. Icy winds whipped doors and windows and found many residents huddling for warmth in front of their stove. But Baba's stove was cold and so was Baba. She died alone and they found her three days later curled up on her cot with several layers of clothes over her.

The entire Barrio was in mourning. The funeral cortege was more impressive than that of a high official and there was actual sadness. Rafa was one of the pallbearers. This was his first encounter with grief and he felt the loss for a long time.

CHAPTER 28

AS HE GREW UP Rafa knew of his father's surreptitious activities and was sometimes called upon to participate by delivering packages he didn't know the content of.

It was a perilous belligerency. House searches were carried out and unwanted individuals were often jailed. Several cells had been uncovered by the Guardia Civil and its members were shot on the spot or taken into custody and executed by a firing squad. No hearing. No trial. Immediate execution.

On a dark September night in 1956 Manólo was confronted by two tri-corned members of the Guardia Civil and two plain clothesmen who made him reveal where Miguel Arroyo lived. Miguel's teachings at the University had been labeled seditious and he was denounced as a clandestine member of the Republican party. They came to arrest him. As the bells of the Iglesia de la Madonna peeled out a quarter to three Manólo banged his chuzo on the sidewalk and clanged the ring of keys in an attempt to forewarn Miguel. At the gate he slowly fumbled through them till one of the officers gave him a shove. *"Andale Sereno!"* and Manólo reluctantly opened the portal. The policemen walked up the stairs, searched the apartment, gathered up a bundle of papers and arrested Miguel to the distress of Yolanda and Rafael.

Manólo watched helplessly as they led him out in handcuffs and they exchanged glances where you could read Manólo to say *"I'm sorry. There's nothing I could do."* And Miguel to say *"I know, my friend, I know"*. Yolanda, hysterical and in tears, stood by helplessly while 16 year old Rafael shook his fist and screamed curses at the uniformed Guardia.

*   *   *

ZAMORA WAS a maximum security prison surrounded by high walls and armed guards in gun turrets. It held inmates whose crimes were far more serious than Miguel's. There were murderers and rapists mixed in with political dissidents.

For the first few days Miguel was locked into a cell with no windows, a mattress on the floor and a pail for toilet purposes. In the middle of the night he was woken up by two guards who tied his feet together bound his hands behind his back and dragged him like a potato sack to an interrogation room. They sat him down on a chair with a bright light shining in his face and two voices shouting at him. *"Tiene que hablar!"* *"What are your connections to last week's terrorist bombings in front of the Banco Nacional de España?"* *"Where did you get the explosives?"* *"Who are the members of your cell?"*

"We need names." The questions came flying out of the darkness on each side of him followed by blows to his back and on his feet. He flinched with every thwack and tears of pain came to his eyes. But he remained silent. This went on for several nights until the guards were convinced that he didn't know anything that might be useful to them.

The next day they moved him to a common cell which he shared with five other prisoners. He was weak and in pain and fell face down on his cot not quite knowing where he was. One of the cell mates came over, lifted his prison shirt and gently rubbed a salve on his back. "You'll be alright Miguel. You'll be alright". The salve felt good and the voice was comforting and familiar. He turned on his back and, through a haze, he vaguely recognized Sendoa smiling down at him. He hadn't seen him since 1942 when he hid him from the Guardia and helped him get away and here they were sharing a prison cell.

For several hours in the afternoon the inmates had access to a large yard where the men milled around. As if they knew what many didn't they treated Miguel with a certain deference. During one of these times Sendoa introduced Miguel to Francis Xavier, a burly man with a thick black mustache, Donato Nastasia, dark skinned with a broken nose, and a rather small older man they just called Maíte who walked with great difficulty. The four of them had been arrested for setting fires in several buildings of the Ministry of Interior. Each had gone through an intensive interrogation with beatings and torture but had not revealed a thing. Sendoa explained that they were part of his cell. "There are many such cells throughout Spain agitating to bring down the dictatorship" he said. "Yes! I know!" Miguel replied.

*   *   *

SUNDAY AFTERNOON was visiting day. Manólo, Yolanda, and Rafael were shown into a fairly large room with barred windows, a table and a number of chairs. Yolanda had prepared some of Miguel's favorite dishes including *chorizos* and a good bottle of wine de Léon. When they showed Miguel in he broke into a smile and didn't know who to hug first, his wife, his son, or his best friend. What was surprising was that they had allowed Sendoa into the room as well.

Sendoa took a piece of paper from his pocket and wrote *"They put me in here because they hope they'll find out a few things they couldn't get out of us through torture. They have a listening device so watch what you are saying."*

Miguel looked pale. His face was drawn. He looked tired and older than his age. Unlike Sendoa, who had been in prison several times before, Miguel suffered greatly from his confinement. He tried to conceal his distress and didn't mention the first three days he had spent in solitary subject to the whims and cruelty of the guards.

By contrast Sendoa looked strong. His imprisonment reinforced his beliefs and he spent a lot of time doing push-ups in his cell to keep in shape and plotting and planning the next coup his unit would undertake. Rafa was impressed. His father's arrest had made him snap and to see him in this condition made him angry and determined to do something.

Sendoa sensed Rafa's frustration and sought to direct his anger to the cause. He took out a piece of paper, wrote something on it and handed it to Rafa. It was an introduction to Alfonso Saline, whom they called El Guerrero so Rafa could form a cell of militants in Madrid which would be an extension of El Guerrero's cell in Bilbao. There was barely time to talk about this and that when the hour was up and the guards took Sendoa and Miguel back to their cell.

*   *   *

ZAMORA PRISON was overcrowded. It was a facility intended for 2000 inmates and there were well over 5000. Miguel had been there a little over three months when the riots broke out. It was never known who started it but everybody participated. They set fire to their mattresses, climbed on the roof of the prison and waved sheets tied to poles with "Free Political Prisoners" written on them.

A large number of police and government troops were called in to seal the prison and quell the rioters and they swung billy clubs indiscriminately breaking arms and smashing heads. Some inmates had knives, others had guns, still others took the wooden planks from their beds and wielded them as truncheons to fight off the guards. Miguel was never a violent person and he found himself caught in the middle.

It took three days to quash the violence and ended with many inmates bloody and requiring medical attention. Ammunition and knives were found in a search of prison cells and the riot ended in a lock down. Visiting days were suspended.

The inmates responded with a sixteen day hunger strike. Miguel's cell mates didn't participate and Miguel became despondent and withdrawn. It seemed as though all the energy which he had in such abundance had been sapped. Sendoa was his life buoy. He held him up in times of stress and cajoled him with false assurances that this confinement would not last. Miguel was not convinced and remained dispirited.

When the lock down ended and the prisoners were again allowed to spend time in the yard Miguel took in the sunshine with relief and recalled Manólo's describing for him the joy he had on seeing the bright sky over Cangas del Narcea when coming up the shaft from the bowels of the mine. He felt the same kind of joy. It lifted his spirit and brought back some glimmer of hope. For some unknown reason Sendoa and Maíte were transferred to another prison.

News of the riot did not make the papers. There were well over 100,000 people incarcerated throughout Spain and the government did not want the disorder to spread so they censored the turmoil. But there was always a grapevine that carried all happenings like leaves in the wind and the riots were the talk of the cafés. Yolanda was in despair. They were without a word from behind the walls and it was rumored that some inmates had been shot. Yolanda feared for Miguel. She worried herself sick. Manólo did his best to sustain her as Sendoa was doing for Miguel. The nights were the worst. She twisted and tossed and couldn't fall asleep.

*　*　*

IT WAS HOT. The temperature had reached 90 degrees for almost a week and it didn't let up at night. The residents of the barrio had all their windows open hoping for a breeze that would bring relief from the intense heat. Manólo walked the night keenly aware of Miguel's absence. He couldn't get the tired look of Miguel's face out of his mind. It filled his nights with anxiety. During the day he spent much of his time affectionately helping Yolanda with her chores, holding up her morale and keeping her from breaking down.

When order was restored at Zamora prison the curtain of silence was lifted and visiting days were reinstated. Yolanda went alone. She walked through the iron gate accompanied by a guard who locked and unlocked a series of heavy gates before showing her into the visiting room. Some minutes later Miguel was brought in. He looked gaunt. The months he had spent behind bars had taken its toll. Yolanda pressed up against him, holding him fast, hoping her love would give him the strength to endure. They talked and held hands and when the hour was up the separation was like a tearing of the cloth. It was that way on every visiting day but it was the day they always looked forward to with so much intensity.

CHAPTER 29

WHEN RAFA TURNED EIGHTEEN he was a student at the Academy just like his father had been and just like his father had been at his age, he was not a boy. He was a man with strong convictions and an underlying anger toward the repressive regime.

Miguel's imprisonment had brought *La Verdad* to a halt. Pastor and Bernardo were demoralized and were persuaded by their wives to abandon the paper and lay low. Rafa took over but he wasn't satisfied with publishing and distributing the paper. He felt words were a slow process for change. He was inclined to more radical action. Bring down the regime by any means Sendoa had said. "Sendoa . . . Sendoa."

The University of Madrid was the constant site of protest and demonstrations frequently turned to violent confrontations between students and police. When the police brought a water canon to bear down on the demonstrators a daring redheaded youth named Rinaldo ran toward them and threw a molotov cocktail. Rafa made him his first recruit.

Nico and Ernesto were twins. Their father Vasco Milan was a scientist and had refused to work on a government project involving chemical weapons. One day he was in the lab wearing the white coat of the researcher when two plainclothesmen came and took him for a ride. He had not been heard from since. The twins' anger was ablaze and they were anxious for an outlet. They welcomed Rafa's organizing for action.

Federico had been in jail twice. Released the first time he escaped the second and was wanted. He was a Córdoban and had heavy eyebrows over an olive-skinned face. He had changed his name and grown a scraggly beard. The lair was a good place for him to hide. He set up a cot in the wine cellar and became the guardian of the hideout.

Rafa was delighted when he found the large cache of arms Miguel and his friends had accumulated well hidden behind casks of vintage wines. There were guns and explosives and the access to the subterranean tunnel added a new dimension to Rafa's militant cell. They called themselves "Los Lobos". The paper remained in mothballs.

*   *   *

CONFRONTED BY GROWING DISCONTENT and in an effort to appease the opposition Franco declared amnesty and freed all political prisoners. Miguel was released and returned home. He was spent and looked older than his 59 years. His hair had turned gray but his eyes still held a passion which survived his two years of confinement and he wanted to bring *"La Verdad"* back to life. The underground paper had been instrumental in uniting the opposition. Since Pastor and Bernardo were no longer willing to take the risk Miguel called upon Julio Borgessa, an assistant professor he had known at the University and suspected of illicit activities, to help him republish and distribute the paper. The printing press and all the implements used in the operation were moved to Señor Borgessa's cellar and Miguel was elated when, several weeks later, "La Verdad" reappeared on café tables and under doorways.

It was a dismal winter. Miguel spent much time in the field and caught a cold. He had a sore throat and was wheezing. Within twenty-four hours he developed a fever and laid in bed, wrapped in a number of blankets, sweating. He had caught pneumonia. He knew the symptoms because his father had been a doctor. Yolanda, remembering her training as a nurse, waited on him with love and affection. Miguel looked up lovingly through the fever at Yolanda and it was as it was some 20 years ago when he lay under a tent in the field hospital and her face was the object of so much emotion.

Miguel knew that Rafa was engaged in belligerent activities and when Rafa sat at his bedside he tried in vain to talk him out of it. Rafa had been brought up as a warrior and he intended to do whatever it took to bring down the regime.

*   *   *

ARTURO BELANDRO never recovered from his two years in the Soviet Gulag. He had become mean. Twice married and twice divorced he lived with his mother Victoria and mistreated her as he had mistreated his wives. His father Colonel Marcos Belandro had died right after Arturo was named chief of the *policía secreto*. He headed death squads made up of members drawn from the military or the police who carried out assassinations and forced disappearances of dissidents and others perceived as opponents of the regime. He relished the brutality of it. Too often death squads wound up massacring innocent civilians in broad daylight just on the basis of some false accusation by a vengeful neighbor.

At first these murders weren't reported in the papers because they wanted to keep the death squads out of the limelight but as the insurgency grew Arturo Belandro thought better of it. Reporting it would serve to frighten the people into submission although the government denied any connection to the killings.

As was their custom Miguel and Manólo met regularly at the Café Bahía, a hotbed of dissent, where the discussion with the men around the table was always about the latest brute violence and how to effectively respond. Marion Bravo never participated. He sat quietly, his shoulders hunched and his face crisped. He had been coming to the tertulia for several weeks carrying copies of *"La Verdad"* under his coat and passing it out to the men.

The waiter brought a round of drinks and they all clinked their glasses to an unmentionable toast. Alejandro Del Norte had a pock-marked face and a bulby nose and spoke with a mixture of Spanish and Catalan. "A squad of blue-shirted bully boys from the Falange's 'Centuria de la Guardia de Franco' armed with truncheons, tire chains and pistols broke into the Workers' Alliance Club last night."

"Yes and they wrecked havoc in the place. They cracked heads indiscriminately. A number of women had to be carried out." Federico was always looking for a fight and was ready for anything. "So what do we do about it? We talk a lot. Talk, talk, talk, but then what?" Marion Bravo bent over, holding his stomach. He was pale and looked like he was about to vomit. He excused himself and ran into the café.

"I have friends in Catalonia" Alejandro said. "They will help us. There are gun runners who come over the Pyrenees from France with automatic weapons and explosives. They are sympathetic to our cause and they would meet us this side of the border." Miguel and Manólo listened but Miguel didn't believe in violence and neither did Manólo. He had tried to convince them that violence leads to violence and nothing could be resolved that way. Manólo was concerned over Marion and went to the lavatory.

There was a screeching of brakes as two black sedans pulled up in front of the café. Four shaded men with machine guns stepped out of the cars and rat tat tat strafed left to right hitting Alejandro, Federico, Miguel and the men sitting at most of the front tables. It took less than sixty seconds and they fell back into the cars and sped off leaving many writhing on the floor.

Manólo heard the shots and ran out to find Miguel lying lifeless under the table in a pool of blood. "No! No! Por amor de Dios!" He fell to the ground and cupped Miguel's head in his lap. Tears ran down his face as he rocked back and forth cradling his friend's face sobbing "Miguel, Miguel, my friend". Alejandro and Federico lay on the other side, either wounded or dead. There was blood all over. Sirens shrieked, people screamed, there was pandemonium and chaos all around.

"Miguel, Miguel, my friend"

CHAPTER 30

THE PORTAL WAS DRAPED IN BLACK. The mourners came from all over. The Iglesia de la Madonna had never held so many people. There was an outpouring of emotions. It seems that Miguel Arroyo's participation in the resistance was whispered on the grapevine and he had many followers who came to pay their respect.

Ignatius Loyola, a roman Catholic priest who had been arrested in a Madrid church and released after three days of confinement, conducted the service. The assembly was solemn. Yolanda sat in the front pew with a black veil over her face, Manólo on one side of her and Rafael on the other. The coffin laid in front of the altar as Father Loyola gave the eulogy in masked terms that only those who knew could understand. The overwhelming reverence everyone bore toward the deceased was to Yolanda a source of comfort in the midst of her grief.

Manólo sat in quiet contemplation. He was not comfortable among all these people. He remembered that he had not gone to Marie-Carmen's funeral nor even to his own father's and he had pangs of guilt. But he knew Miguel longer and better than he had known Pépé and he was part of the family. He suddenly realized that if he hadn't gone into the Café to check on Marion Bravo he would have been a victim as well. He wondered why fate had intervened on his behalf and he was allowed to live.

When the service was over the mourners filed out and the coffin was placed in a black horse-drawn hearse which the mourners followed to the cemetery. Manólo, Yolanda and Rafa stood side by side as the coffin was lowered into the grave and a fine rain started to come down. Yolanda sobbed under the black veil and Manólo put his hand on her shoulder to comfort her.

Rafa looked into the grave and seethed with anger at his father's murder. He looked up and his eyes fell upon Marion Bravo standing in back among the mourners. He didn't like Bravo. He was an odd fellow and Rafa didn't trust him. His mind suddenly raced and he began to connect the dots. The way he had heard it Bravo had gone to the lavatory when the shooting took place. He wasn't in the line of fire. He must have known. He must have fingered them. Rafa had had his suspicions for a while but had nothing to go on. Now he knew and Bravo was going to get his.

A few days later Marion Bravo was killed in a hit and run accident. The driver was never caught.

*   *   *

MANÓLO WALKED THE STREET wearing the night like a shroud. He crossed the Plaza San Ramón and stepped into the church. It was empty and Manólo kneeled in front of the Madonna with his head in his hands and tears streaming down his face. He looked up at the Virgin Mary as if to ask her why she took his friend from him but she looked down on him with beatitude.

"Miguel Arroyo" he had said. "And you?" That's how the long enduring friendship had started. It all flashed through his mind.

"Can you read Manólo?" "Yes" "Then take it!"

Luisa, the Contessa's daughter and the love shared between the three of them. Cortez and Adolfo and the days spent turning the mimeograph machine in back of Miguel's compound. The time when they worked together to hide Dolores Ibárruri, La Pasionaria. And when Miguel came back wounded from the war and introduced him to his wife Yolanda and the tinge of jealousy he had felt at having to share his friend. The arrest of Miguel that gruesome night and the visiting days at the Zamora prison. And Miguel's head in his lap at the last. Something he would never forget. Manólo rose to his feet, went over and lit a candle in his memory then walked out of the church despondently.

* * *

MARION BRAVO had been an inside man. He worked for the *policía secreto* and the death squad that had committed the massacre. When Rafa found out that Arturo Belandro had given the order which resulted in

232

the killings he was infuriated. Death squads had murdered thousands of Spaniards in the past few years, and now they had murdered his father. He clenched both fists in anger. Sitting at his desk under the lamp in the hideout he composed a declaration:

MANIFESTO

"TAKE NOTICE that the Spanish people will no longer tolerate the outrages committed upon them, the arrests, the imprisonments, the torture, the killings that this repressive government has been guilty off. From this day forward, every act of violence perpetrated by the government will be avenged, one for one, blow by blow. LET THIS BE FAIR WARNING!"

Viva España
Los Lobos

The Manifesto was nailed to the ornate front door of the City Hall much like Martin Luther's Manifesto of Protest had been so long ago. It was also pasted on walls all over Madrid and in other cities, placed as broadsides on café tables and under doors and it made a splash of major proportions. It was an outright declaration of war.

*　　*　　*

THE CHURCH BELLS RANG THREE when Rafa showed up with Nico and Rinaldo in front of the general store several cuadras away from Arturo Belandro's residence. Rinaldo held a satchel full of explosives and they huddled in the darkness of the doorway. Within minutes Manólo appeared and they walked briskly to the compound. The street was quiet. Manólo reached for the key on the ring and opened the portal. In the courtyard stood the brand new SEAT sedan Arturo Belandro had received as a gift from the Minister of the Interior Enrique de Borbon.

Manólo stood watch as Rafa and Rinaldo fiddled around with the engine to wire the car's ignition system to explode when the car was started. Every now and then a noise jarred them and they winced. Sometimes it was someone talking in his sleep. Sometimes it was a cat shrieking on the rooftop. Each unexpected sound gave them a jolt. It took longer and was harder to install than they had expected. Nico suggested they affix the explosive device to the underside of the car. The slightest motion would detonate the explosive and blow the car and its occupant to smithereens.

When they were done Rinaldo put all his tools back in the plumber's kit and they quietly walked out. Manólo locked the door behind them and they disappeared around the corner. A clap was heard in the distance and Manólo headed in the direction from which it came.

* * *

LA PRENSA
MADRID
September 13, 1964

ARTURO BELANDRO ASSASSINATED

Arturo Delmar Belandro, head of the policía secreto, was killed last night when a bomb which had been placed under his car exploded.

They didn't leave a calling card but the police suspect that a militant anti-government group called Los Lobos were responsible for this heinous act.

THE MANIFESTO was the talk on the streets and in the cafés all over Spain. It was a call to action and brought together the diverse cells who took on the name "Los Lobos" and considered young Rafael Arroyo El Lobo, their nominal head.

* * *

"MANÓLO GARCÍA!"

Manólo stood up. He and three others had been called into police headquarters for questioning. "You are the Sereno of the Barrio Viejo?" Capitàn Gonzales asked.

235

"Si Señor."

"It has come to my attention that your barrio is a bee's nest of insurgency." Manólo tried to keep a calm face despite the tremor that was going through his body.

"I am sorry Señor but I have not observed anything suspicious. I have been the Sereno in this neighborhood for nearly 50 years. I know every resident. I can only say that they are all law abiding". Manólo's hands were by his side but his legs were shaky.

"What about Señora Arroyo, the widow of Professor Miguel Arroyo?"

"She grieved herself into silence and hasn't spoken since" Manólo lied. "She doesn't go out and I think she is incapable of serious activity."

"What about her son?"

"I haven't seen him in over six months. I think the death of his father caused him to fear for his life and he left Madrid."

You could tell that the Capitàn wasn't satisfied but he turned his attention to the two other Serenos. Several hours of questioning did not bring out anything the Capitàn could go on and he dismissed the three Serenos with disdain. Manólo had gone through this kind of interrogation before but the stakes were higher now and he went home relieved that it didn't go further.

CHAPTER 31

VICTORIA BELANDRO had had several mental breakdowns over the years and when her son was killed she went berserk. The men in white came and took her in an ambulance to an asylum on the outskirts of Madrid.

Yolanda's loss of Miguel was just as traumatic. Everything in the house reminded her of him and she spent many hours crying softly into her pillow. Manólo was there for her as much as for himself. They comforted each other in their grief. To keep herself from falling apart she returned to nursing and took a job at the Hospital de la Paz. She knew what Rafa was doing and she cautioned him to be careful which didn't prevent her from worrying that he might get caught and be shot as had happened so often these violent days. With much coaxing she convinced him to get away for a while, to lay low and calm the storm that raged inside his soul.

* * *

THE TIMES HAD CHANGED. Railroads were faster and it made traveling easier. Rafa took the train to Bilbao in the Basque country. He sat by the window and looked at the typical Euskadi landscape. It took his mind off the weight of his decision at twenty-four to spearhead Spain out of the stranglehold of fascism. There were miles and miles of lush green pastures interspersed here and there by a village with church steeples inhabited by storks standing high in their twig nests and fanning their young with great wings. There were horse drawn covered wagons all along the way. The gypsies were on the road trekking north for their annual gathering at Sainte Marie des Mères, on the south coast of France. The train clattered along with a steady rhythm and Rafa recalled his father telling him how he and Sendoa and another man whose name he didn't remember had taken part in the blowing up of a train full of ammunition during the civil war.

When the train pulled in at the station in Bilbao with a long and loud whistle and steam gushing out of its engine, a typical fine Basque rain they call "txirimiri" was coming down. Rafa made his way to the depot and took a bus to Durango. The thirty minute bus ride made him nervous. He didn't exactly know what he came for. A rest and a quiet time was only a pretext. He knew there was more to it and he had yet to find out what.

* * *

AT A KIOSK at the terminal he bought the Euskadi Diario. The paper was full of the latest attack on Franco's summer residence in San Sebastian, a bomb which shattered the windows and collapsed part of the roof. The raid had been conducted by members of Euskadi Ta Askatasuna, commonly called ETA, an extremist wing of Basque nationalism.

Rafa had left the rain in Bilbao and the sun was shining bright in Durango. He sat at a café and ordered a glass of the Basque cider. The three or four men standing at the bar must have been hanging around all morning and they looked at Rafa with suspicion. Everyone more or less knew each other in Durango and Rafa was a stranger. They looked and huddled and whispered. Rafa folded his morning paper and walked over to them.

"Buenos dias Señores"

"Buenos dias Señor" they replied.

"Do you know a man named Sendoa Vazquez?" he asked.

The men looked at each other. The question brought frowns of concern as if it should not have been asked. The older one with the slick black hair parted in the middle shook his head. From the wary look on their faces Rafa realized he was treading on thin ice and they needed an explanation.

"My name is Rafael Arroyo. I came from Madrid. My father Miguel fought alongside Sendoa during the war. I haven't seen Sendoa in a long time. I was hoping . . ."

"You are the son of Miguel Arroyo?" they interrupted in astonishment and recognition. They took off their beret, shook Rafa's hand and warmly embraced him in turn. It was a big secret for the government but anyone who was on the underground grapevine knew Miguel Arroyo had been the publisher of *"La Verdad"*.

Miko, a strapping young man with bushy hair, lowered his head. "We were sorry to hear about your father. Shot down in broad daylight. *Que tragedia! Que pérdida!* He was a candle in the dark and his underground paper ignited candles all over Spain and gave us hope of bringing down this repressive regime. In addition to the candles that were lit in his memory" old man Pablo said mournfully. He took his glasses off and rubbed his eyes. "Quite a few others were killed in that raid".

Rafa put down his glass. "Alejandro Del Norte, Federico Baltazar, and Julio Borgessa who had been my father's right hand man" he said. "His 17 year old son Cisco who had nothing to do with the paper but was just there to keep his father company took two bullets in the chest but survived. Then there were innocent bystanders who were just sitting at the front tables when the men in black started blasting away. I wasn't there but the scene repeats itself in my dreams and I often wake up screaming."

"What will happen to *La Verdad*?" Miko asked.

"When Cisco recovers from his injuries he will be vengeful enough to take over the printing and distribution. There is no way in which *La Verdad* can be silenced."

"And you?"

"I know Sendoa Vazquez was a firebrand. I met him many years ago and my father spoke of him often. I need to refresh my ideas so I came to meet with him."

At the mention of Sendoa's name their expression changed to one of sadness and they all bowed their heads. There was a heavy moment of silence. A few months ago the government had taken extreme measures to bring the Euskadis in line. They arrested teachers and local officials and many of them were never seen again. ETA launched an attack against police and army units and a vicious cycle of violence and counter violence followed. Sendoa was right in the midst of it. "He is also no longer with us. He was killed in an encounter with the police in December."

Rafa shook his head in disbelief. The men recognized Rafa's distress. They slapped Rafa on the back and offered him a glass of the popular Sagardoa or cider wine. "Ah! Joven! Life can be hard and unpredictable. We lost a good man. We were like brothers. Solidarity, friendship and brotherhood are not mere words with us. Euskadis close ranks in the face of danger and Sendoa was always up front when things were happening." Rafa shook his head in disbelief. "He died fighting for what he believed in. He died in battle. But your father didn't believe in violence and he was murdered". They ordered another drink. There was renewed anger in Rafa and it went through his body like a flash. The men noticed.

"What will you do now?" Miko asked. Rafa didn't know what to say. Sendoa was his connection to Durango. He didn't know anyone else.

"I'll probably take the train back to Madrid in the morning." Then he remembered Sendoa's mention of Alfonso Saline, the one they called El Guerrero. He would have asked about him but he didn't think it appropriate. He might decide to stay and look him up.

Miko took Rafa's glass, put his arm around his shoulder and they all walked out and sat down at an outdoor table. The plaza was decorated with red, white and green banners. "Now that you're here you must see how we celebrate Easter Pascua in Pais Vasco and you are in for a treat". After several glasses of cider wine which made them a little tipsy and brought them closer together, Rafa asked about Sendoa's mother. "She's a strong woman. She can take the blows and rebound with spunk. I'll take you to her if you like" Miko offered. Rafa nodded enthusiastically.

* * *

THE HOUSE WAS UP A NARROW ROAD to the Baserri, farm house. Mamà Irune was in the garden tending her flowers. She was a strong woman. Euskadi women were known for their tenacity. In many households they were the matriarch. She had outlived her husband and had seen her youngest son Enrique fall under the bullets of government militia in a public execution. And now she mourned the loss of her eldest son Sendoa. The dogs barked and she looked up as Rafa and his companion turned into the yard. "Miko who is your friend?"

"This is Rafael Arroyo. He's from Madrid. He knew Sendoa a long time ago." That's all he had to say. Mamà Irune set down her hoe and came out to greet them. Lines of sorrow were permanently etched on her face but her smile remained warm and friendly. They went into her kitchen and she brought out a bottle of Rioja which they sipped while Rafa talked about Miguel and Sendoa and told the stories his father had repeated to him many times over the years. He was afraid that it might make her sad but she seemed to take pride in her son's doings. She was a fervent Euskadi and knew her son was exposing himself to danger for a cause she and most others firmly believed in. She liked Rafael and invited him to stay for supper and spend the night in a room over the barn.

The clamor of bleating sheep was heard coming from the field. "It's my daughter" Irune said "she's bringing the sheep in from the pasture." "KATALIN" she shouted out the window "come on in here". With cruddy boots, a loose blouse and a long skirt, Katalin stood in the doorway holding her shepherd's staff. She was in her late twenties with piercing dark eyes and, quite unusual for a Basque woman, long cascading black hair which reminded Rafa of his mother Yolanda. But she looked a lot like her brother Sendoa and she wore the committed look of the Vazquez family. "I lost my sons" Irune said "but I still have a daughter". Katalin nodded and Rafa held out a hand which she shook firmly.

The diner was something more out of Manólo's past than Rafa's. Rafa was an only child. So was Miguel before him and he had been used to sitting down at the table with two people, occasionally four. But at Mamà Irune's they came from everywhere and everyone was a cousin. No one was ever invited. They just came. Mamà Irune was a good cook. The table was always covered with food. There was garlicky fish soup, jamon serrano and roasted pimientos, and many odd dried dishes, an astounding variety. The "cousins" all helped themselves. Everyone ate with gusto and glanced at Rafael who was sitting next to Mamà Irune. Rafa in turn kept looking at Katalin from across the table and when she noticed she smiled an invitation which he wasn't sure he recognized.

Mamà Irune rose and struck her fork against her glass to get everyone's attention and raised it on high. "I have taken the blows but my heart is filled with hope. On this Aberri Eguna let us drink to Euskadi and to our beloveds who stood up for her, for us, and for Spain. To my sons Enrique and Sendoa and to Miguel Arroyo the father of our friend Rafael."

There was clinking of glasses and loud shouting of approval and Katalin looked over to Rafa who accepted the accolade with unpretentious humility.

Before the evening was over Mamà Irune talked Rafa into taking Katalin to the fair and to the dance that followed. Rafa didn't need much convincing. He had been admiring her beauty and her strength throughout the evening meal.

* * *

ABERRI EGUNA is the day of the Basque homeland. Franco had banned it and severely persecuted those who celebrated it. But it always fell on Easter Sunday and the Euskadis marked the resurrection of Jesus Christ with the rebirth of a people who had found themselves and their destiny. They disguised their celebration under the cloak of Pascua.

Easter Sunday began with the Txistulariak processing through the streets before the morning pilgrimage to the shrine of Our Lady of Begonia and a communion service. This was followed by a large outdoor mass. After mass various dance groups paraded through the streets performing here and there. The streets, plazas and balconies filled up with people anxious to watch the procession go by.

In the evening hundreds of Fallas, colorful papier-mâché statues, were put to the match and the flames lit up the sky as firemen stood by just in case. The dance that followed took place at the community hall. An accordion, a guitar and a tambourine provided the music to enliven the festival. The women brought their men from the Siderias cider houses and the dancing was lively and spirited. Rafa brought Katalin. She wore a red skirt adorned with richly textured brocade and a brooch attached to a black velvet choker. Several strands of beads, elongated earrings and an embroidered ribbon at the end of a braid made her look stunning. She had grace and Rafa was captivated.

The music was exuberant and joyously unrestrained and Katalin danced with wild abandon. She wasn't the only one. Everyone did. Few words were exchanged between her and Rafa but it was clear that they were made from the same cloth and it brought feelings to the surface. Still neither of them showed their emotions. It was as though showing was a sign of weakness. But the emotions were there and he knew it and so did she. Rafa began to think that Katalin was the reason he had come to Durango.

CHAPTER 32

RAFA SPENT SEVERAL DAYS in Durango guided by Katalin. She brought out feelings in him he had forgotten he was capable of. He had to remind himself that she was Sendoa's sister. On the third day while Rafa helped Katalin herd the sheep she came out with "You know that Sendoa was a member of ETA don't you?"

"Yes!" They had never spoken about it but he knew without her telling him.

"There's a meeting tonight. I'd like you to come. There's someone I want you to meet."

She borrowed a bicycle from a cousin and the two of them pedaled in semi-darkness across town and up the hill on the other side. As they approached the stone building on the gravel road a loud and continuous oinking was heard. "He raises pigs" Katalin explained.

There was a light in the kitchen and six men were seated around the table arguing. When Katalin entered with Rafael the tall one stood up, walked over and gave her a hug. He was dark skinned and had the look of someone who isn't afraid of anything.

"Alfonso, this is Rafael Arroyo from Madrid. His father Miguel was a friend of Sendoa's". A smile of recognition came on Alfonso's face.

"Your reputation precedes you compadre. I'm Alfonso Saline" he said stretching out a hand in a brotherly greeting. "Your name has been bantered around for quite some time and tied to Los Lobos. We have been at war with the government for a long time now but your call to arms has brought many factions together."

Rafa didn't know whether he should be pleased that Los Lobos was known among the anti-Franco militants or be concerned that outsiders might also know of their activities. Alfonso pointed to a heavyset man with a round face and a kerchief around his neck. "This is Mauricio. The one with the red hair is Samuel and the ones squabbling over there are Ignacio and Zeru. We've been arguing over the next hit maybe you can settle the argument. We are in the same business after all."

For the next three hours they talked about their cache and how to use it with maximum effectiveness. Katalin participated with vigor and it was clear that she wasn't just a guest. Rafa looked at her with admiration. They had recently gotten a large stash of weapons and explosives from a successful gun running operation across the Pyrenees and were plotting another target. Most of the targets were in the capital. A strike in the provinces would not be as dramatic. Their targets were always government buildings and they tried to avoid civilian casualties. It would not be long before their next strike.

* * *

LA PRENSA
MADRID
May 18, 1969

Four bombs exploded in a week in the streets of Madrid. An explosion shattered the headquarters of the Guardia Civil and a portion of an administration building on the Via Grande. This is one of many acts of terrorism that have been taking place throughout Spain in the past week and the army has been called in to respond. Insurgent groups who are interconnected appear to coordinate these attacks. So far no one has claimed responsibility.

* * *

MANÓLO STOOD IN HIS SMOCK on the raised platform, with the ring of keys around his neck, leaning on his father's chuzo. At 72, though slightly bent, he still embodied an image of strength. His face was lined but his eyes were intense and the years he spent in the arms of the night gave him a mysterious look that might be compared to the look in the eyes of the Mona Lisa. Vittorio Sol peered out from behind the canvas, paint brush in hand. Maybe it was that look that he had seen under the street lamp that night.

When Arturo Belandro was killed the Belandro residence was sold. Vittorio Sol, an eccentric artist of the impressionist school, turned the part of the premises which gave unto the sunny side of the courtyard into a studio. When the workmen came to repair the damage caused by the explosion, Vittorio Sol had them install three large skylights which brought in the clear white light of the morning sun and the soft yellow light of the late afternoon.

Vittorio Sol was robust. A flamboyant character with the red rugged face of a stone mason and the hands of a miner. The scarf and the beret were the only things that allowed him to be identified as an artist. He was a serious painter and was often up at daybreak working in his studio. In mid-morning he would come out of his compound in his paint-stained smock, a beret and a red bandanna, and walk to the Café Gijón where he would sit and sip a hot rum and read the morning paper. He was reclusive and didn't socialize with the people in the neighborhood or say more than a few words to the waiter who served him at the Café.

On an occasion when he came home late at night and clapped and Manólo appeared with his keys, he pulled him into the light and looked at him with discernment. He held him there for a moment. "Sereno, do you make enough money to live on?" he asked.

"I manage Señor."

"Would you be willing to pose for me? I find your features interesting. I would pay you of course Sereno."

So now Manólo spent portions of his day in Vittorio Sol's studio standing on a platform while the artist looked out from behind the canvas with his palette and his paint brush. During the three weeks of his posing there was little or no conversation between them and Sol never asked his name and addressed him only as Sereno. Actually that's what he was painting, not Manólo but the Sereno.

One session, during the break, Sol offered him a glass of wine. It was a first and Manólo wondered why. The reason soon became apparent. "Sereno" Sol said "you know most of the people in this Barrio. Can you think of anyone that might be interested in posing for me after I finish your portrait?"

Manólo thought a bit. "Yes. I think some of the girls at Spanish Kate's would be glad for the extra money. Never mind that they have a degree of vanity and would love to see themselves on canvas".

"Will you speak to them for me?"

"Yes. I will"

And for the next few months Marcía, Jasmin and Coretta, the new ladies of the night took turns on the platform and were captured in the impressionistic paintings of Vittorio Sol.

When some time later Vittorio Sol opened his studio to the public and a number of art critics and some members of high society filed into the courtyard to see his latest works, "El Sereno" the beautifully framed painting of the dark night watchman was the center of attraction and received the greatest acclaim. No one asked who the model had been.

CHAPTER 33

RINALDO TOOK OVER Rafa's cell and with Federico and the twins Nico and Ernesto they were at the source of many of the so called acts of terrorism. Other groups took militant action throughout Spain. "Terrorism" Rafael growled under his breath. He thought of himself as a freedom fighter, a revolutionary. "What if the German people had resorted to violence against the Nazis? What if Adolph Hitler had been assassinated? How different things would have turned out". This last thought stuck to the back of his mind and was filed away. The militia was everywhere. So was Rafa. He traveled the country from Córdoba to Cadiz meeting with leaders of "the resistance" and helping coordinate activities between cells. He was in constant danger but he maintained his composure and everywhere he went people covered for him.

The government took drastic measures. The Guardia Civil was placed in every factory throughout Spain. They clamped down on all activities. Groups were not allowed to congregate. When more then three people got together it was considered unlawful assembly and they were arrested. Suspected members of an anti-Franco underground were taken in a raid in the Ricon section of Madrid and eight dynamite cartridges and a mass of subversive literature was discovered. There was also a secret radio station and police searched frantically for a hidden transmitter that jammed government newscasts and broadcast anti-fascist propaganda.

The Barrio Viejo had seen its day. The moneyed denizens had moved to newer more opulent private residences on the other side of the city. That made the barrio a working class neighborhood and fear permeated every compound. Manólo was 74 and still walking the night with the keys jangling from his neck. He had realized long ago that his anonymity in the barrio, where the residents looked at him as their guardian but where no one knew his name or who he was, was a great asset but he was getting on and was no longer active in the cell. He spent much time worrying about Rafa.

The Guardia Civil stopped people randomly on the street and asked for their I.D. They managed to get several camouflaged truckloads of cartridges, flame projectors and machine gun belts. Caches were found almost everywhere the police looked. They also went on house to house searches trying to root out the enemies of fascism. On several occasions Manólo had to divert their attention in different directions when they seemed to be headed for Rafael's hideout.

The newspapers read:

"The wave of terrorist bombings continues unabated".

By contrast the posters, broadsides and flyers had a variety of messages to support the anti-Franco movement: *"Simón Bolivar was a liberator not a terrorist". "Augusto Sandino was a revolutionary not a terrorist". "One person's terrorist is another person's patriot". "Pancho Villa and Emilio Zapata were rebels not terrorists".* Viva España! Los Lobos.

* * *

GENERAL HEBERTO BELAROSA sat upright and looked at the men seated around the table. He had recently been appointed deputy by Franciso Franco himself to put an end to the uprisings and had summoned these men for a strategy session. There was Capitàn Gastón Martinez an army officer in charge of putting down strikes and riots, Julio Valiente the Comandante of the Guardia Civil, Fernando Almari the head of the death squads, and several other members of the government, all high level law and order officials. Each had a file on illegal activities they had uncovered and the actions they had taken.

"Señores we're not getting anywhere. These terrorists are doing a great deal of damage and we've lost a number of valuable people. We must bring together the various organisms for a concerted action to put an end to these atrocious activities." His face was flushed.

The door opened and Santiago del Campo came bursting in. "My apologies Don Belarosa. I am late but

I have good news". Santiago del Campo was the head of the *policía secreto.* "We've arrested an informant and persuaded him to talk. We now know who is at the head of Los Lobos". All the men perked up. "His name is Rafael Arroyo and they call him El Lobo. He is the son of Miguel Arroyo who was a professor at the University and was himself an anti-government agitator. He was fired and ultimately put down with a bunch of other agitators. His son Rafael Arroyo has taken the mantle and he is far more dangerous than his father ever was".

Don Belarosa seemed pleased. He had a satisfied smirk on his face. "Do you know where he is and have you arrested him yet Santiago?"

"Regretfully we have not. But we know who he is now and he can't hide forever."

"He must be found. He is more than a thorn in our side, he is a veritable threat to the regime. We must cut off the head of the snake for the uprising to fall apart.

"We are putting on a massive hunt. We'll get him Don Belarosa rest assured".

*　　*　　*

MANÓLO SAT ON THE COUCH surrounded by knickknacks and pictures on the wall. He spent a lot of time in Yolanda's apartment when she was at work at the hospital. It was warm and pleasant in contrast with his dark and dingy lodgings. Miguel's presence was still there among the books and the curios and it made Manólo more aware of the emptiness within himself, a void Miguel had filled for so long. He got up and walked over to the bookshelves. They were stacked with books Miguel had read. He picked one at random and sat down on the couch again. The front door opened and Yolanda walked in. She was still in her nurse's uniform and smiled at Manólo. She had kept a remnant of her beauty through the years but she looked tired. Manólo got up and kissed her on both cheeks.

"You're home early".

She sat down on a chair, took off her shoes and rubbed her feet. "They came for me at the hospital".

"Who?"

"The *policía secreto*. They took me to their headquarters and questioned me for hours. They wanted to know where Rafa was. I told them that he had moved out two years ago and that I didn't know where he was at this time. It's true but I don't think they believed me".

She took off her nurse's cap and hung it on the coat rack. "Rafa wouldn't tell me so I wouldn't feel I am giving him away if I'm questioned as I was today. But *you* know where he is Manólo. I know that you know". Manólo turned away without saying a word. Yolanda went into the kitchen and came back with two glasses of wine. She handed one to Manólo and sat down next to him.

"Rafa calls me now and then" she sighed "but he knows the house is watched so he never shows up. Once in a while, on market day, he appears at the stalls alongside of me. We talk without looking at each other. Sometimes he touches my hand and I want to take him in my arms and hold him. I know what he's doing. I knew what Miguel was doing too. But Rafa is a wanted man and I fear for his life."

"He is probably numero uno on their list".

"They asked for a picture of Rafa. It sounded like they don't know what he looks like".

"Did you give them one?"

"No! I told them Rafa was camera shy and didn't let anyone take his picture".

Manólo looked lovingly at Yolanda. There was still so much sadness written on her face. "Don't you think you should retire from nursing?" he remarked.

"If I did what would I have left? You and this place which constantly reminds me of him? My job at the hospital makes me feel alive. I see people every day who are suffering. Many of them are amputees from the Civil War. The prosthesis they have been wearing is primitive at best. It is made of leather, wood and metal and their wounds have become infected after so many years. When I see them I am grateful I am whole. And above all my job helps me forget that, while they have lost a limb, I have also lost the best part of me. And you Manólo? Don't you think it's time YOU retired?"

Manólo didn't answer.

*   *   *

"THIS MAN WANTS TO SEE YOU CAPITAN". The tri-cornered Guardia Civil brought him in. The man was disheveled, wore a torn brown coat and was missing an arm.

"Who are you?"

"My name is Rico Capitàn and I think I have some information you want".

"Alright. Let's have it".

"Well you see . . . I'm a poor man and . . ."

"Alright, alright. If I like what you have to say you'll be rewarded". The man was trembling and fear was written all over his face. Capitàn Morro reached in his pocket, pulled out a pack of cigarettes and offered him one. "Calm down now. Nothing bad is going to happen to you. Just tell us what you know".

The man took the cigarette, put it in his mouth and waited. Since the Capitàn did not move he pointed to the empty sleeve of his missing right arm. Morro struck a match and held it up to him. The man took a deep drag and seemed to relax a bit. "The word on the grapevine is that El Lobo, Rafael Arroyo is headed for Castellón. That's all I know".

CHAPTER 34

THE TIMES WERE RIGHT for revolution. Workers and peasants were fed up with being exploited but outright revolution was not possible because the government had the army, the police and the well armed Guardia Civil. Violent protest and sabotage were the only means of resistance.

Rafa was desolate. Before leaving Madrid Rafa had heard from Rinaldo that the twins Nico and Ernesto had been caught with explosives in their knapsacks, taken to the armory and shot in the courtyard each leaving a grieving widow and children which would have to be provided for. It made him sad but it also made him angry and it reinforced the path of violence he had chosen. *"Every act of violence perpetrated by the government will be avenged, one for one, blow by blow."*

* * *

RAFA GOT OFF THE TRAIN in Castellón and looked around. He had come out of his small cell to become a major organizer with cells all over Spain. The platform was crowded. Soldiers with rifles seemed to be everywhere. People entering or leaving the station had show their ID to security guards posted at the exits.

Rafa had come to meet with someone but he didn't know what he looked like only his name, Rodrigo, and that he would wear a red bandanna. His eyes searched among the people who were standing around and spotted him near the food vendor eating a black sausage. He was a nondescript individual with the look of an accountant, small sunken eyes and dyed black hair combed across his balding head. Not at all what Rafa had expected.

He walked over to the vendor and ordered a black sausage as well. Looking away he chanced "Rodrigo?".

"Yes. Rafa?"

"Yes".

"Welcome to Castellón. As you can see the place is crawling with police".

"I didn't expect this kind of reception. How are we going to get out of the terminal Rodrigo?"

"Just follow me" and he started to walk toward the exit with aplomb. Rafael followed closely behind. As he got to within 5 feet of the security guard he suddenly turned and screamed *"ALLA ESTA!"* "There he is!" pointing at someone running to catch the train which was pulling out and starting to run after him. The security guard blew his whistle loud and he and several members of the secret police started giving chase.

In the confusion that followed Rodrigo turned around and walked Rafa out the unguarded exit. Rafa was astonished at Rodrigo's craftiness. A black SEAT was waiting by the curb and they both got in. An intense looking young man in a dark shirt was in the driver's seat and took off at full speed.

When they were at a certain distance from the railroad station Rodrigo introduced the young man. "This is Guido. His father and his uncle disappeared over a year ago and he is still seething". Then, turning to Rafa, he shook his hand greeting him as he had wanted to when he first met him at the sausage stand.

* * *

THE SIX MEN were lined up against the bullet ridden stone wall. They had been arrested for sedition and spent the last 48 hours being interrogated, beaten, and tortured. The firing squad stood at the ready.

"Do any of you have any last words?" the Sargento called out. He was tall and pale under his military cap. It was the first time he had been ordered to take charge of an execution and he dreaded what he was about to do.

One of the men whose face was smashed and whose left eye was half closed took a step forward, proud and defiant and shouted aloud "Si!" The Sargento stood back. "*I AM EL LOBO*" he declared. He had barely finished than another man mutilated by the horrendous torture they had all sustained stepped forward and shouted *"I AM EL LOBO"*. And another and another. *"I AM EL LOBO"*

"Ready?"

"El Lobo is everywhere".

"Aim!".

"Wherever there is a man who stands up against tyranny there is El Lobo. VIVA ESPAÑA!"

"Fire!"

The six men became known as "The Martyrs of Castellón".

* * *

RODRIGO WAS A PHOTOGRAPHER and lived behind his storefront studio. The display window had pictures in sepia brown of a wedding couple, a newborn infant in the arms of its mother, and a girl in her first communion dress. All peaceful scenes of warmth and love. His studio and dark room were in the cellar. An enlarger on a table in the center and cameras and photographic equipment all around. Under the table there was a rug and under that rug there was a trap door with a fairly large space where explosives, dynamite, and other arms were stored.

Now five men gathered in the dark room under the small red light of the black curtained developing area. There was Rodrigo, two men who were called Diablo and Perro, Guido, and Rafael Arroyo. During the forty years of the Franco dictatorship, the government had complete control of all forms of the press and media. Strict censorship was exercised and dissent was not tolerated. Their primary object was incapacitating the radio station that broadcast government propaganda. It was located just outside Castellón de la Plana on a hill overlooking the town.

Rodrigo took out a number of photographs he had taken of the radio station with a powerful telescopic lens and it was agreed that arson would be the best means to accomplish their purpose. When the discussion was over and the plans were firmed up Guido expressed his anguish over the recent execution of "Los Mártires de Castellón". The tension that immediately tightened the room was full of rage and fury. They decided to add the police station as one of their targets. In the 48 hours that followed Rafa met with over a dozen other militant young Spaniards.

By the time Rafa left Castellón. a fire had destroyed the radio station and the police headquarters building was in ruins. In the wake of the execution of "Los Mártires de Castellón" a series of fires and bombings followed uninterrupted throughout Spain, from Valencia to Cadiz, from Córdoba to Oviedo.

CHAPTER 35

IN JUNE 1972 Franco, his health failing, appointed Luis Carrero Blanco prime minister. Blanco was opposed by many for stifling popular dissent. He embodied hard-line Francoism and was seen as someone who would carry on the Caudillo's hard-line dictatorship with arbitrary arrests, disappearance of dissidents and government condoned death-squads killings.

Opposition to the regime mounted. A wave of strikes spread across the country and rebellion in the universities caused Franco to proclaim a "state of exception" throughout Spain. The rights to freedom of expression and assembly were suspended. Ten leading opponents of the Franco regime, one of them a Roman Catholic priest, were arrested in a Madrid Church and were accused of unlawful assembly and "insolence to the forces of order". Despite the fact that their offense was minor, the government sought to make an example of them.

The leaders of the opposition to the regime called on all workers and students to show their support by staging demonstrations and stoppages of work in protest against the political trial. Thousands of angry demonstrators campaigned against the case and clashed with police. In the past year Franco's regime had been assaulted by disaffected priests, workers, students and members of the Basque minority whose leader, Eustaqui Mendizabel, was killed in a shoot-out with police in April. Alfonso Saline, alias El Guerrero, succeeded him.

*   *   *

THERE WAS A BIG HUSH in the courtroom as the defendant Marcelino Camacho was brought in flanked by two armed members of the Guardia Civil. As the well-known Socialist trade union leader he was the central figure in this trial. He was a big man with a prominent face and a big nose. He walked tall and proud. He had been in trouble with the police before and had spent time in jail on several occasions, often having been picked up in random street round-ups.

The courtroom looked like a small indoor amphitheater. The Palacio de Justicia was usually a criminal court with a single judge impressively dressed in his black robe and cap sitting on-high looking down at the accused, but this was a military tribunal. Three high-backed red velvet chairs had replaced the bench and high-ranking army officers sat in judgment. The press was kept out. Only two carefully chosen right-wing reporters and a small crowd of Francist were allowed to observe.

Marcelino Camacho stood quiet and defiant in a ten foot perimeter of empty space. He looked around for his comrades but they were not there. Outside on the street thousands of sympathizers were staging a peaceful demonstration of solidarity with the accused. The courthouse was surrounded by a massive force of the gray uniformed armed police who were just looking for an excuse to come down on the demonstrators. When a small group of angry young men threw stones the police went at them with flailing truncheons and a number of heads were bashed and a number of arrests were made.

In the courtroom the atmosphere was stark and sinister. While Camacho stood at the bar the Guardia brought in the other defendants, the worker-priest Father Garcia Salve wearing his cassock, and eight other prominent opponents of the Franco regime, two of them women. All of them had been savagely interrogated for days and clearly showed signs of torture.

The court officer dressed in a Napoleon like uniform struck the parquet three times with his ornate staff and everyone rose to his feet. From the side door came the judges. They climbed the steps to the bench and took their seats. The president of the tribunal General Guillermo Brigante had personally been selected to preside at the trial by Franco himself. He sat down pompously between Colonel Sylvestro who had fought with the Nationalist in the civil war, and Comandante DePalma the head of army intelligence. After calling the court to order the General looked down at Marcelino Camacho standing alone in the dock.

"You are charged with sedition, unlawful assembly and conspiracy to overthrow the government. What have you to say for yourself?" There was irony in his tone. It was a question that almost didn't expect a valid answer.

Camacho took out his handkerchief and blew his nose loud and long. Then he looked up at the President. "Every self-respecting Spaniard who loves his country is standing at the dock alongside of me. I am but the symbol of their resistance. If I am guilty of treason so are millions of others who are out there in the cities, in the country, on the farms and in the factories. YOU ARE THE ONES WHO SHOULD BE ON TRIAL HERE".

General Brigante was livid. "Your disrespect for this tribunal is not going to help you in this courtroom."

"Respect must be earned Mr. President" Camacho replied. This exchange of words continued for a while then Camacho was asked to sit down and a number of false witnesses were called to testify. The trial was just for show. The outcome had been decided in advance. The only thing that came as a surprise was the sentence.

After a brief deliberation the defendants were called before the bench. One after the other they stood in front of the panel of judges as General Brigante handed down six death sentences and more than 700 years of prison. The Spanish people were outraged and took to the streets. The trial got international press and protests took place all around the world.

*   *   *

ALFONSO SALINE DETERMINED that drastic action had to be taken to rid Spain of the oppressive dictatorship and called a meeting of leaders from throughout the country.

The meeting took place in Durango. Rafa came from Asturias where he had been sheltered by friends of Manólo. Rodrigo came from Castellón, Vicente from Cadiz and Diego from Tarragona. They met in Alfonso Saline's hideout, a root cellar that had been dug out in back of his barn to make a fairly large underground chamber. It was covered with straw and the access was through a trap door in the pigpen so knee boots were necessary. It was low-vaulted and there was barely enough headroom in the lair so Saline, who was fairly tall, had to keep his head down when standing. Light and air came through a pipe in the ceiling of the chamber. The oinking of the pigs had served him well when on several occasions unwanted official visitors came unexpectedly.

There was a table, chairs, a lamp hanging from the ceiling, and a barrel of Euskadi wine up against the wall. The five major players in this struggle were backed by Saline's operatives, Mauricio, Samuel, Ignacio and Zeru, virulent members of ETA with many acts of sabotage under their belt, from cutting brake fluid lines and slashing tires on military trucks to blowing up Franco's summer residence in San Sebastian.

There were glasses on the table and they all filled them from the spigot of the wine barrel. Saline was the first to speak. "I've brought you together because things can't go on like this. The prisons are filled with innocent people whose only crime is criticism of the government's stranglehold on the Spanish people. There's only one answer to our problem" Alfonso said "We have to get rid of the Caudillo".

"You mean assassinate him?" Vicente snapped.

"Can you think of something else?" The room became silent. The idea of assassination had never come up.

Rodriguo shook his head. "There is no way in which we can get close enough to Franco to kill him and in any case, he is old and sick and is really no longer making the decisions."

"Rodrigo is right" Diego said "Franco is not the problem any more. Luis Carrero Blanco is the one we must bring down." There was much discussion but there was no longer any question that assassination was the answer. It was only who would be the victim and in the end all agreed Carrero Blanco, the aging dictator's hand-picked successor, would take the fall. They were convinced that the assassination would quicken the end of fascism in Spain. Now it was only a matter of when and how this would be done.

They constructed an elaborate scheme. For several weeks Rinaldo, Federico, Samuel and Zeru took turns monitoring the day to day activities of the Prime Minister, watching the itinerary he took daily, making notes as to where he stopped for a cortado, where he got a haircut, down to the minutest detail of his comings and goings crucial in the planning of his assassination. Blanco always had a bodyguard with him and gunning him down was not an option so they decided to use the sewer under the streets of Madrid. They would set up explosives along the route Blanco took every Sunday after mass at the Iglesia San Francisco de Borgia.

CHAPTER 36

CALLE CLAUDIO COELLO was lined with neat little houses with small well-tended front yards. It was the street Admiral Carrero Blanco used regularly on Sundays coming back from mass. Rafa and Saline walked up to No. 113 and rang the bell. A maid in uniform opened the door.

"Señores?"

"Doña Calderon esta en casa?"

"Just a moment please".

Shortly an elegantly dressed dignified lady appeared in the doorway. Rafa bowed and introduced himself. "My name is Pedro Salazar and this is my colleague Manuel De la Cruz. We are interested in renting your house at No. 104 across the way. I am a sculptor and my friend here is a painter. We are from Cordoba and we are preparing for an exhibit at the Galería del Prado."

Doña Calderon was a patron of the arts and she was impressed. "I'll get the key and show you the premises". The house was spacious with a foyer, a salon and a large drawing room on the ground floor. Saline walked over and looked out the window. He noted that there was a good view of the street and you could see quite a distance. Doña Calderon took them upstairs and showed them the bedrooms and the bathroom. As they walked back downstairs Rafa asked "Do you have a cellar Señora?" Most houses in this fashionable neighborhood did. From the pantry in back of the kitchen a door opened on a staircase leading down to the cellar. The space was fairly large and dry.

"I am glad it isn't damp down here" Saline commented. "It will make a good storage space for my paintings". On the far end Saline noted the bolted door. He knew what it was but he wanted to make sure so he pointed to it. "That leads to the sewer below Señor De la Cruz" Doña Calderon said "it hasn't been opened in years". Rafa and Saline looked at each other and nodded. It was an essential element of what they needed for the plan.

"I think this will do fine Señora".

*　　*　　*

A WHILE LATER, drinking tea in Doña Calderon's sitting room 'Pedro Salazar' and 'Manuel De la Cruz' demonstrated their knowledge of the arts in an exchange which Doña Calderon visibly enjoyed.

"How long will you be needing the apartment?" she asked.

"Probably for six months".

"It will be a pleasure to have you as my tenants" she said.
I hope you will invite me to the opening reception".

"You can be sure of that. It will be a privilege to have
a patron of the arts as our guest". Doña Calderon perked
up at the compliment.

*   *   *

WITHIN THE NEXT FEW DAYS Mauricio and Samuel
came furtively carrying boxes marked art supplies but
which contained explosives, detonators and everything
that was needed for the job. It was all taken down to the
cellar and the cache was covered with a large canvas.

Rafa broke the lock of the door leading down to the
sewers and Ignacio and Zeru spent days in the sewer tunnel
surveying, examining and combing every nook and cranny
for a suitable place to plant the explosives. They were both
bomb experts and had extensive experience blowing up
marked targets.

Saturday the 19th of December was a cold day. It was
colder still in the sewer under Claudio Coello Street. Rafa
and Saline wore heavy garments and joined Ignacio and
Zeru below ground. They set up a massive one hundred
pounds of plastic explosives at a selected location next
to anti-tank mines obtained from gun runners. The

mines were wireless and, unlike conventional explosives requiring cables connected to a detonator, they were capable of being detonated by remote control. It was a sophisticated plot, as intricate as any that were recorded in the history books.

Then the Sunday came.

*　*　*

BBC NEWS REPORT—20 December 1973

SPANISH PRIME MINISTER
ASSASSINATED

The Spanish Prime Minister, Admiral Luis Carrero Blanco, has been killed in a car bomb attack in Madrid. The 70 year old, his bodyguard and a driver died instantly and four other people were injured after a remote-controlled bomb was detonated as he passed.

The massive explosion sent the car hurtling into the air and over the roof of the San Francisco de Borga Church where Mr Blanco had been attending mass.

Police said the killers had placed a bomb in the sewer tunnel under the street the admiral used regularly on his return from mass and triggered it from an opposite basement in a well-planned assassination plot.

No group has yet claimed it carried out the attack.

CHAPTER 37

THE WINTER OF 1973 was a hard one, cold, snow and sleet. Manólo had arthritis in his right leg and when it acted up he dragged it along. He would have retired long ago but he had no children, no one to turn the ring of keys over to. And where would he go? He had no family left in Asturias. His family was here in the barrio, Yolanda, Rafael, and the extended family of his flock, the residents of the barrio. He was their parent.

The night was quiet and the streets were calm. Manólo leaned against the wall of a house that hadn't been lived in for many years. He touched the keys around his neck as he had done so often and wandered dreamily into the dwellings he was the guardian of. He felt the large key with the ridges along the side and remembered the last conversation he had with Rafael. "I am going on a mission. It is a dangerous mission but it is something I must do if Spain is to be free. When it is done I will go with Saline to his family in Durango and you will not see me for a while. Meanwhile you have the key to the storeroom. In the desk drawer you will find the list of the compadres and instructions on who to contact to clean out the storage, remove the guns and explosives, destroy the books and dismantle the hideout."

Rafael was the son he never had and he loved him. If that key were to be found Rafa, Saline, and all the others would be shot as terrorists. He couldn't bear the thought and felt the silence behind the empty walls he was leaning against. To quiet his apprehension he let his mind wander through his past and the times long ago in Asturias when the sky was a silver blue, hearing the laughter of children playing in wide open fields and reveling at all that was now but a memory.

A distant clap clap caught him dozing in the doorway, shaking him out of his warm embracing dream. It startled him and he waited a moment to hear it again and pinpoint the spot it came from. Though his eyes had become weak with age his ears were still sharp. It came from the other side of the barrio. That's strange he thought looking at his watch. No one comes home from that direction at 2:30 in the morning.

Not knowing how long he had been dozing he hurried to the spot and found the street deserted. No one was waiting. Then clap clap was heard again. This time from the furthest corner of his bailiwick. Thinking that he heard it wrong the first time he forced his old legs to quickstep through the whole length of the barrio and came upon another deserted street.

Confused and bewildered there was another clap clap from somewhere far off and the faint sound of laughter. "It's those kids again" his mind told him. Having nothing to do on a Saturday night these young ruffians played tricks on the old Sereno keeping him running from one end of the barrio to the other to answer an anonymous clap clap. It was a cruel joke but he forgave them their youth.

Then he collapsed.

*   *   *

Small item on page 4

LA PRENSA

MADRID
January 12, 1974

The Sereno of the Barrio Viejo was found dead in the Calle d'Oro last week. He had no successors. The Council of the Elders is looking for a replacement. Interested parties should present themselves at the Town Hall on the Plaza San Ramón

*   *   *

IT WAS RAINING. Ignacio walked the wet naked street in a drenched poncho and sloshed around the puddles in deep crevices of the sidewalk that hadn't been repaired in years. He did not feel the loneliness Manólo had felt.

Despite the fact that his leather shoes were soaked through and through and his feet were wet he was lighthearted and pleased with himself. Several of the elders had commented on how good a job he was doing and it made him burst with pride.

As the rain got heavier he stepped beneath an overhang and looked down upon the keys he protected under his slicker fingering them lovingly. He had gotten to the point where they were like friends, friends he knew and recognized, each having a companion door, a perfect counterpart. But one of them was like a stranger to him and he jerked back. Despite much effort he had not found its match, the door that it was meant to open, and it weighed around his neck like a cannon ball, the weight of failure, of incompetence, of not living up to the trust the elders of the council had placed in him. It gnawed at his insides and in utter frustration he took the ring off his neck and removed the offending key. It was heavy in his hand and he looked at it questioningly as if the key could talk and tell him where to go.

The rain continued. There was thunder and lightning and it cracked like a whip. The gushing water flowed like a river in the gutter. Ignacio stood in a doorway and watched the water run down the sewer. Suddenly, trying to remove the pain the mysterious key was causing him, he stepped out of his shelter and dropped the key down the drain. It made a clanging sound as it went down and the rain stopped.

A clap clap was heard in the distance. It echoed through the streets. Ignacio struck the wet pavement twice with his chuzo to indicate that he was coming and walked out of the light of the street lamp into the darkness.

THE END

EPILOGUE

Rafa, Saline and their accomplices were never caught and the assassination of Carrero Blanco was the last nail in the coffin of the crumbling fascist regime that the people of Spain had endured for 34 years under the yoke of the 81 year old Franco's dictatorship.

ABOUT THE AUTHOR

Jay Frankston was raised in Paris, and came to the U.S. in 1942. He became a lawyer and practiced in New York for 20 years reaching the top of his profession and writing at the same time. In 1972 he gave up law and New York and moved to California where he became a college instructor. He is the nationally published author of several books some of which have been condensed in Reader's Digest and translated into 15 languages. His book "A Christmas Story" a true story has been read by millions and included in numerous anthologies from Germany to Korea and beyond.

Edwards Brothers,Inc!
Thorofare, NJ 08086
24 May, 2010
BA2010144